The
Successor
of the
World

Ashish Laxman

Become
Shakespeare
.com

First published in 2018 by

Becomeshakespeare.com
Wordit Content Design & Editing Services Pvt Ltd
Unit - 26, Building A-1, Nr Wadala RTO,
Wadala (East),
Mumbai 400037, India
T:+91 8080226699

This book has been funded by WORDIT ART FUND
WORDIT ART FUND helps deserving
Authors publish their work
To apply for funding, please visit us at
becomeshakespeare.com

©
ISBN : 978-93-88081-04-7

Cover design & Concept: Abhas Sinha
Abhassinha1@gmail.com

Author Photograph: Nipun Chawla
inipunda@gmail.com

Other Short Stories by Ashish Laxman

For the life & times of Mangalore

Chapter 1

The dawn was charming, in the sense of being nascent; the nascency when you have woken up too early and the droopy leaves of a tree outside assure your thoughts. That grey air. It was pleasant too, so pleasant that the denizens may misremember the city they had slept in the last night.

He stepped out of his mansion – 'The Nirvana' at the Rajpura Road, in front of the dense Ridge forests. *'The Stewarts' would have been a suitable one,* he sometimes thought glancing at the wall, particularly at the scribbled name slab that always left an impression of a funeral, mainly because it had almost no other word on it. Though, 'Nirvana' itself is a fairly popular word which means an ideal state of harmony and end of sufferings.

Here I am. I will be driven again to that place thirty miles away; these sparrows overlook me doing it every morning.

It wasn't that early.

1

A tall statured person with spectacles never does things randomly, at least it is presumed so; he always gives an impression of having infallible plans, but this man had none, no plans at all. The only planned thing ever inflicted on him was the surname – 'Stewart'. Audin's father, George Jonathan Stewart, a business tycoon, was a devout Hindu like Audin's grandfather though the family hailed from England, and had been living in India for the past centuries.

Audin's education had been fundamentally English. Early years were consumed in studying at the Catholic School of London where his grandmother taught, but later, fulfilling his father's spiritual aspirations, he came to India at the age of twelve in 1994, and was schooled in Delhi since then.

There was a car, a white Mercedes, parked outside, near the gate, gracefully. This gate almost deserved a Mercedes; other gates in this locality are nothing but iron fillings taught to behave well but this one looked like it had that innate ability to personify itself whenever a human neared – a doorman himself.

"Good morning, Sir," the driver greeted, half awake.

It was monsoon, and the wet road appeared newly blackish. The bulky Neem had dropped its oldest, yellow drupes on the road, its only contribution to the beauty of this day. It is during this time, after dawn, when one imagines himself walking on the road barefoot, trampling the thin mirrors of water after the drizzling has stopped and its fresh scent has manifested comfortably. But Audin was unconcerned. "I may not go."

"...Sir, but, you look nicely dressed though," The driver said casually, whiffing away the irritating dust particles, unaware that there weren't any, from the car's neat glass.

I don't know what the purpose of this gentleman's life is. Who wouldn't wonder? He should return to his country, marry a girl, and have children - I would have done that undoubtedly.

"I haven't bathed for two days. The dress is too nice to tell you that."

"...and Rama...?" the driver wanted an immediate confirmation if it was another idle day for him, just like yesterday, and the day before as well.

"You need not drop him to the mills at eight. Get him here, if possible." Audin said, and left for the neighbouring Ridge forests as if he were never to return. He left every place in this inattentive gait that sometimes beggars display when they are determined to sleep. But, in his own mind he was readying himself to share his daytime with today's strangers.

If I can catch a fish today that doesn't like water. He was often heard saying so about this world.

'Strangers' here most probably suggests those people on whom Audin tested his atheistic ideas leisurely – those numerous, plain, unique humans that go unnoticed if you don't stop to hear what they are murmuring to themselves.

Rama was one of the fishes, the oldest stranger, now the closest friend, a school mate, and a farmer's son who was born in a village sharing borders with the capital.

Audin, on weekends, and other 'busy' days, discoursed with Rama on 'valueless' ideas like - life of fruitless plants, or illusioned soldiers, or terminologies of religious cults. A biographer would have painted Audin as a champion of elenctic debate who denuded the opponent of his wit, leaving him stranded like a victim of frost-bite.

This forested area has a sincere historical importance; it was once used as a hideout by freedom fighters of India against Audin's ancestors, or more fondly, the British Raj.

"You don't care to understand, eh? It's easy. I can't put myself up at home to watch your feats. People work for their living, even I." Rama, also, was one of the workers at the Stewarts' mills; he had been working his fingers to the bone to raise the profits. The only way he recreated himself on holidays was cursing; cursing his fate for everything from hair fall to the tax on a restaurant bill. He found it amusing. For him a day off only meant staying at his not so homely home and paying extra attention to his wife's words.

I mind repeating things. Listen whenever I give you a chance to listen. She said to him the last Sunday. He usually plagiarised her commands to use them on the mill's employees – it was another subtle form of recreational cursing.

He got married at the age of eighteen, haphazardly, after his mother's demise, who wished to see him married when she was in her death-bed. Audin convinced Rama on the occasion that the marriage would help him evolve as a human, and it was not a pale consummation of his past deeds; *the dead past was just equally useful as a safe broken into.*

"I would have done something fruitful at this hour. You should have informed me the last night."

"Uh, yes, but that wouldn't have brought you here." Audin asks Rama to sit down; poor visibility all around.

"This time of day is the *Brahma Muhurta*; the mind is most active at this hour, apt for meditation & prayers, you waste such a precious hour in talking this gibberish, which you are about to."

"You would have been with your wife had I not called you here. Snoring, probably."

"I wish I could bless you with a few thousand wives, just like Vaisravana!"

"I see you haven't stopped the monthly subscriptions of those mysterious, religious books."

Rama seated himself on the dewy grass near the periwinkle flowers, the grass that had sprawled herself all around on the unattended regions as if she was looking for the face of the sky, watching the white clouds, and thanking them for what they had been.

"See, uh, I respect that you are an artist, but I don't understand this escapism." Rama said looking upwards.

"I am trying to create an exclusively new philosophy that helps people escape the struggle of life."

"You cannot *create* anything. God hasn't given us the power to create anything. We can merely rearrange the existing ideas, or imitate ideas in nature."

"Who said that?"

"Jatharu Rishi."

"That's absurd."

"It isn't hard to understand. Imagine a new animal that doesn't exist. Nothing that exists!" Rama began talking like a learned scholar.

"Alright."

"What did you imagine?"

"A flying ox with two legs, one big eye, three tails."

"You just rearranged. Ox exists, legs exist, eyes exist, tails exist..."

"An animal made of bricks jumping like...."

"Bricks exist!"

"Mermaids. They don't exist."

"Women exist!"

Audin had never had any female intrusion in his life. He had postulated for himself: *A women is more complex than her own DNA structure, excessively twisted but seemingly parallel; the wanting of such an illusionary being in a male's life justifies only biological obsession and no intellectual impulse.*

"It is so desolate at this hour." Audin justifies the noiselessness.

"Of course it is! People have work to do; people abide by the rules of time and they must."

"It is because they have to work for someone else. I do what I like, and it is, of course, a matter of chance. I am free." Audin stood up triumphantly, and threw a mass-less stone on the reflective surface of the lake. A green ripple surfaced.

"That's dangerous. That is called 'Vikarma' – misusing your freedom to do work carelessly, against the laws of nature, such work gives a you body of a low animal in your next birth."

"What's a low animal? Lesser height?"

"The problem lies in the fact that you are just another lazy bastard who thinks of himself to be a gem, waiting for the crown to come and pick him up. That's the problem, like that stone that thinks it can swim across the water on its own and always sinks down to the bottom." Audin threw another stone that crossed the lake just grazing the motionless water.

"*Matter of chance.* Neither the thrower, nor does the stone know where they are heading to."

"I may swim, and I may sink. I may cause another ripple or perhaps I may hit another stone. As deep a mystery as life, does the result even matter?" Audin concluded, standing akimbo, as if he was waiting for stone's assent on this note.

"Then, why throw the stone?" Rama came back sharply.

"That's why I still haven't solved the backyard mystery. I just want to retire from life without having to go through any process."

"The backyard mystery? The backyard mystery." Rama seemed to have forgotten about it in all these years.

"You are the only one I have told whatever I knew about it, aren't you? And we would do something about it." Audin confided in Rama more than he did in his father or anyone else. Rama had been a proud registrar of Audin's ledger of secrets ever since he met him.

"Life is indeed so; I may swim; I may sink; I may cause a ripple or perhaps I may hit another stone..." Audin repeated, echoing in the dense woods, loud enough to attract attention of one of the busy gardeners- Bhola Prasad, who retorted, "And you may also hit those innocent ducks! You life-sucking white pig! Run away now or I will kill you with this scythe!"

Bhola Prasad was a gardener here for ages; he could only inherit the famous scythe from his father. His wife had run away with his brother a month after their marriage, two years ago; the reason he told Audin was he wasn't as spendthrift, and potent, as his brother and had not been able to make her happy which he could, and thus, casually substantiated Audin's theory on women. Audin possessed this seductive virtue of coercing people to vent out their guilt in front of him helplessly, which he later innocently revealed to anyone who merely asked. Since that day, the gardener had been wishing for his death and been cursing him to impotency.

But Audin advocated the Socratic answer, for he was stubbornly inquisitive – "*When we first start facing the truth, the process may be frightening, and many people run back to their old lives. But if we continue to face it, we will eventually be able to handle it better.*"

The two friends were crossing the road back towards home, the traffic sparse; A rare sight for a Delhiite. Rama saw a mob gathered near the front gate of the mansion- mobs generally give a pessimistic feeling, and a long white vehicle, which was another rare sight - for Audin had very few friends and Mr Stewart kept the business outside the tall walls.

"There is something...I don't..." Rama struggled to raise his vision to look beyond.

A heavy man slumped on a stretcher was being carried by two men out of the mansion; quite a *funny* start of the day. The heavy man was Audin's father, Mr Stewart himself, and the long white vehicle was an ambulance from the nearest hospital. Rama ran. Audin could still not feel the panic, his slow reaction time to be blamed for this, which had struck all of a sudden on everyone else around him - why panic is so mesmerizing no one can answer.

A slow man sees the world as it is. A running man always sees a world running away from him in an opposite direction - how would such a man catch a contrary thought thrown at him? Be slow to be steady.

"Is that an ambulance?" Audin's pace quickened a little bit to hear what Rama was blabbering to nobody. He saw his mother too, she had been crying.

Mrs Stewart was a perfect mother and wife. She, after all, was solely responsible for Audin's Indian upbringing, which her husband deeply wanted. She was a lecturer of Hindi language when she met Mr Stewart at a literary seminar. He was one of the sponsors of the event, and was bowled over by her flawless diction of the language and her sculptural beauty.

"Where have you been? And why didn't you pick your phone up? Look at your father!" The air around Mrs Stewart, and her ricocheting words, seemed to have been spawned by a wrecked boat rocking in a cold-blooded ocean. "Look at your father...!"

Audin rummaged through his pyjamas but couldn't find the device; he never cared for his belongings and called each one of them compulsory distractions, "I left it there," he said to sweating Rama, as if the seriousness of his mother's question was only directed at the phone's presence. Rama shouted, as the ambulance drifted away, "Get the car out!" he swerved the car out of the house racing towards the hospital, for the driver had already left having been instructed to do so by Audin himself. Audin was now a little surprised to see his strong father lying on a stretcher like a helpless new-born, as he had never seen him in such an irresponsible state before, but he was composed, certainly more composed than a usual man would be at such a scene.

Death is an established organisation which has a monopoly on our breaths.

"How did this happen?" Audin asked sitting in the back seat, as if he was one of those distant relatives that mainly show up at deaths and anniversaries.

"He was reading the newspaper at his breakfast table; he suddenly fell off his chair. He wasn't breathing. I tried to call; you wouldn't pick up the phone..."

People in this city, those who are drivers, all but every one of them feel very lonesome on roads - this reflects as soon as their tyres touch the asphalt, and they drive as if no one around them ever existed; a strange Brownian motion where each particle is running into another in sheer melancholy. Somehow, the speedy Mercedes of The Stewarts reached the hospital dodging the lonesome drivers.

"He is all right, a feeble paralysis attack; don't queue up here like this!" An arrogant doctor came out of the emergency ward. By then, the news of Mr Stewart's paralysis attack had already clouded the news channels; he was after all an influential personality and a favourite of the interviewers; relatives and acquaintances had started gate-crashing.

"Oh my God! What happened? I was watching the news and it came to me..."A sad well-wisher had just arrived. "It's nothing; just a chest pain. Please leave. There is nothing to worry..." Rama took charge of handling the crowd.

"What? Chest pain? My father had the same. He was...I must tell he was..."

"No! Sir, you must not tell. I am not an event manager, or a suggestion box. Do I look like as rectangular as a suggestion box? Show your rehearsed concern to that man, the ward boy," Rama got furious. The religiously orthodox and fidgety personality of Rama blew the air with restlessness wherever he went, living quite paradoxically up to his name.

It took them hours to meet Mr Stewart in his secluded room. He looked as normal as a bruised child from the neighbourhood. "I am good." He waived his left hand at his wife. He couldn't move the right one, his entire right-half body in fact.

"They are saying you would be like this..."

"I know. I know that. They say it all the times. Even you said that once..." He smiles with Audin, instead of getting up from the bed passionately and asking his son to accept the world the way it is.

The sun started slipping down towards the west. Audin was chosen by Mr Stewart himself, to accompany him for the night.

"Do take care of your mother when I am not there. You will?" George wrote on a chit, as he was not able to speak effortlessly; perhaps he was not feeling as good as doctors concluded or as he pretended. Audin could sense his lack of experience in saying something appropriate for the moment, "Yes. Yes, I will, certainly," he hesitatingly said scratching at the iron railing of the bed.

Audin stood by the window; the sky was sprinkled with stars, and some colour of moonlight.

I think I should start behaving well; I am nearly thirty years old. Perhaps, there should have been a rule book for all these situations where you are not allowed to explore much on your own - The book of general life.

Traffic outside was shining more than the lit hoardings. An unhappy household lady was bargaining with a yellow auto-puller; a bus stop was still jostling with keen passengers; an intimate couple was strolling creatively, and a million other confused silhouettes were appearing and disappearing from the scene as if they were at a magician's table.

I am indebted to my father and I must return the debts; there are many who, at this point of time, are indebted to my father and they must be praying for his death, but I must realize my duties towards him. He has indeed been a great man.

Audin kept quizzing his brain about the irony of death, and about himself, till midnight. Mr Stewart had an urge to ask him to sleep as well; he wrote on a chit and threw it aiming at Audin's back who didn't notice any movement about him. He finally called out, "I can't sleep with someone standing at the window murmuring. Audin, sleep!"

Audin laid himself on the grey couch where so many people had slept before. It was very clean and sanitized but smelled of a tin roof.

"Are you writing in this diary?

"I will stop writing, if you sleep..." Mr Stewart didn't want to let go of the pen.

"You are writing with your left hand. Is it so unstoppable? This expresses urgency."

"I can't move my right body; you know that." Audin abruptly switched off the lights to force George to put his pen to rest.

Audin soon, expectedly, went into a deep slumber. Mr Stewart was continuously looking at Audin, still writing with the stagger of the friendless hand. He always kept this small, personal diary, supported by a tiny pen, close to him. The milky light coming out of the glass was enough to dishearten the darkness, and assist him to see his son's face that had changed a lot in the last thirty years.

He pushed himself sideways, and caressed Audin's hair.

You have been irritating, but good.

George Stewart had a strange, certain feeling of not waking up tomorrow morning, and thus it was the last time to talk to his son.

You are a young man, no signs of wrinkles, a pure heart, and a fresh mind. You will be unstoppable, my son; more fast than my pen.

Audin didn't hear anything. He was in a peaceful dormant state; a tear eventually fell on his forehead; a suppressed tear that was churned out of the emotional pit into which Mr Stewart had fallen. A strong man at heart, perhaps that's why it was not a cardiac arrest; he was mentally readying himself to bid farewell to the family, to dissolve all the bonds of love. He covered his mouth to stifle gasping and ungovernable tears. There was no one to pacify him, and to ask him about the foreboding. There was no one to tell him that he is not going anywhere.

"Uh! I have smudged the paper; look at the ink; he won't be able to read it," Mr Stewart told himself, bleary eyes "And if he doesn't read...no, no, no, that would not be a very good thing to say..."

He signed the diary at 3:00 a.m. and stowed it inside Audin's pyjamas along with the favourite ink pen.

A dressed up nurse came in after two hours, bound by his duty, nearly awake, much like a beautiful but constipated air-hostess at an early morning flight. The flurry was on the way; elevators had begun the to-and-fro journeys, the cleaning department had regained its senses, the parking lot was piling up, and the shops encircling the hospital were rolling their shutters up. No one knew until then that Mr Stewart had died, and that he knew he was going to die, and that he had wept all night.

Audin had woken up after hearing alert doctors trying, futilely, to put his father on oxygen. The 'soul' had abandoned the body and the pulse had become intangible; the "symptoms" of death. Audin realized that he was in a hospital and he had come here last night to stay with his father. He had made a promise to his father that he will take care of his mother. And doctors had concluded that he was out-of-danger. Audin wanted to call her, and Rama, but he had no phone in his pyjamas and only a diary bearing his father's name, and a pen seeping the ink profusely as if telling him that he was the witness.

George Jonathan Stewart was cremated at the local crematorium, as per Hindu ceremonies, on the same evening. Most of the newspapers had the similar headline- "The beloved philanthropist businessman, George J. Stewart, dies of a paralysis attack at 58." Audin was not reading the newspapers; he had something else: the diary which his father wanted him to read. He was reading what was being written, before him, last night. The smudged pages of the diary had all the answers and a few questions too.

Chapter 2

7000 BC.

No one has ever been able to stop the revolving wheel of time - whose beginning and end is unknown; undefined rather. The wheel is timeless itself, as if Satan's own vicious circle. The '*Dvapara Yuga*' or the age of energy is approaching its end. Less than twelve hours are left and proceedings for the final rituals have already begun.

Sage Paramhamsa is sitting on the bank of The Ganges along with his seven surrendered disciples; one of whom will be throned as *the successor of the world*, before midnight, for a span of ten thousand human years. And probably, it will be '*Anutaapa.*' The mere thought of separation from their spiritual master has eclipsed the glory of receiving this mark of honour. For them, their master, who taught them the most sought after secrets of spirituality and mysticism, is going to depart in the next twelve hours from this Earth forever and leave one of them to continue his legacy.

The seven Disciples - *Anutaapa, Prtikshit, Suyojit, Viharama, Aravityea, Yaksham, and Bhuvamsa*, were cherry-picked by Sage Paramhamsa during his pilgrimage around the Earth a hundred years ago to patronize them for the rest of their lives and to become a potter of their destinies, to shape one of them into a life-saving pot that would quench the thirst of unfortunate waterless souls. This long period of tutelage has made it unbearable for the disciples to bid him farewell.

The deserving Anutaapa

Sage Paramhamsa found him in the southern parts of ancient India when he was a child of nine years. Although born to a farmer's family, his sense of reasoning soon outclassed that of the fellows born as Brahmins. He was rearing his cattle on the grasslands when Paramhamsa passed by; seeing such a young child administrating a big herd, he went near and asked, "Do these holy cows belong to you?" Anutaapa knelt down to greet the anonymous sage and replied, "O great saint, I am grazing them, and I do this every evening. They belong to my uncle."

"I want one of those cows for my ashram, and, in return, you will have these precious jewels." Anutaapa handed Paramhamsa the healthiest cow.

"I want one more." Anutaapa unhesitatingly gave another one. Soon Paramhamsa had all of the cows on his side, and asked the composed boy, "You have sold all your cows without the owner's consent; what if your uncle doesn't accept the jewels and wants his cows back?"

"Since I have not asked the owner, if I sell them I will be called a thief, and thus, I am not going to take those jewels from you. I have donated, O great sage, for which the owner will never deny. As the one who donates a cow gets the eternal bliss and knowledge as it is said in Vedas." Hearing these sane words out of a nine year old child, Sage Paramhamsa at once decided to make him his first disciple. "O my dear child, you are too intelligent for your age; you must come with me and I shall give you the real jewels of wisdom."

The final Dialogue

Anutaapa: You know the future, and, you are the knower of the past. I am ignorant. Please reveal to me what I have done. Why have you banished me from your servitor-ship? I must have committed the most formidable sins! I must have disobeyed you! O Great Saint! Please reveal to me!

Sage Paramhamsa: Neither have you committed a sin, nor have you disobeyed me at any time in your life. You have pleased me on all occasions. But I can feel your uneasiness, for I have felt the same when my master departed and handed over to me the crown. Now, it's your turn.

Anutaapa: How will I survive without you, O great teacher! The pain of separation is unbearable; it will, certainly, eat away my soul and my body, like vultures nipping a carcass.

Sage Paramhamsa: You have served me with all your heart, with devotion, and surrendered unto me yourself. Remember, always, I have not only chosen you over the six, but over the entire world to become the successor. You are the wisest of all; you have defeated the great Indian philosopher-*Dviraja*, at the age of seventeen. Who but you can do justice to this crown? Realize your dormant capabilities; you have the mind and the strength of several humans put together. You will soon realize that you are the right, and the only one, to be my successor. This will be your repayment for the tutelage.

Anutaapa: O reservoir of mercy! Since you have instructed me for the repayment, I, without saying another word, accept this responsibility. For a Guru, a disciple must, at any time, be ready to do anything; as *Eklavaya*, the great archer, at once gave away his right thumb to his master. Now, I urge you to acquaint me to my duties and character for the rest of my life.

Sage Paramhamsa: The Holy Vedas give a nice description of the '*Apaursheya*,' or the godly successor, his characteristics, his duties and his importance. I will recite to you a verse:

With his wisdom leaves, Apaursheya enlivens the dead; it is how you unite the nature's law. The wisdom leaves immortalize.

With his wisdom leaves, Apaursheya heals the festering wounds; it is how you unite the nature's law. The wisdom leaves immortalize.

With his wisdom leaves, Apaursheya shivers the strong Earth; it is how you unite the nature's law. The wisdom leaves immortalize.

With his wisdom leaves, Apaursheya lulls down the heavy floods; it is how you unite the nature's law. The wisdom leaves immortalize.

With his wisdom leaves, Apaursheya pacifies the worn heart; it is how you unite the nature's law. The wisdom leaves immortalize.

Anutaapa: Is the age to come such an age of distress and turbulence? How long will it continue? O my Master! How will I use my powers to protect the sacred religion?

Sage Paramhamsa: This will be the age of darkness. The religiousness, truthfulness, cleanliness, tolerance and mercy, as well as duration of life, memory and physical strength will decrease. Ridiculers of God will be the new preachers and will create false doctrines. The most corrupt will rule the state. Prostitution, gambling, and selling intoxicative substances will be considered as decent businesses. Poverty will be taken for something unholy. Hypocrisy, and jugglery of words, will be considered as intelligence. One's outer appearance and coiffure will qualify for being beautiful. Marital relations will be too ephemeral. A promise will be enough to have sexual contacts. Women will start dressing like men, and will be unchaste. Men will be lusty, greedy, and will eat unrestrictedly. Vegetation will be reduced but pre-cooked food would be readily available. The age of humans will not go much beyond fifty.

Among this vast ocean of pain, violence and lamentation, you will differentiate between the just and the unjust. You will re-establish people's faith in God. You will, for the next ten thousand human years, stay on Earth to rekindle the extinguished fire of religiousness.

Anutaapa: When would this merciless age of '*Kaliyuga*' end?

Sage Paramhamsa: Kaliyuga will be there for 432,000 human years. Many successors will appear on this holy Earth after you, and many have before you. This Master-disciple relationship has been continuing from the sun deity who passed on the eternal knowledge, for protection of mankind, to his disciple. The long tradition has now arrived at the threshold of Kaliyuga, after passing through three Yugas, and unto you.

Anutaapa: What, in the age, would mark the end of my regime? And I will have completed my duty.

Sage Paramhamsa: When the same constellation, as of today, falls again, and you will have grown ten thousand years old, soon after, your successor will appear.

Anutaapa: I will, as you desire, help protect the path of righteousness. Kindly render me the eternal knowledge, O great Sage! I bow down to you.

Sage Paramhamsa: I hand over to you the chest of powers, the wisdom leaves. The timeless wisdom leaves! They are crafted out of the condensed ether, which, in its empty form, fills the space and becomes black, and holds all the universes together. No such thing will ever be created again. The soil of Earth is the hearth of many valuables like gold, rubies and diamonds– which shine the most and attract humans; like uncommon herbs that can cure any disease; like tasting the ambrosia which makes the humans immortal for an entire Yuga, and many more. But not even one of them is as glorious as the wisdom leaves.

Anutaapa: O slayer of ignorance! Instruct me what I shall not do; the forbidden actions.

Sage Paramhamsa: O Anutaapa, this is the instruction of the most importance, as the power rendered to you also makes you the most vulnerable to commit sinful actions- hear it by your heart.

You must practice the three qualities- Truth, compassion and penance.

You must eat and drink only as much as you need, as much as is enough for you to survive, and that too by begging, even though knowing that you can manifest the best of the edibles by the wisdom leaves.

You must not accept any disciple throughout your journey.

You must never be proud of yourself, and be as humble as a dust particle.

You must not possess any material object except a 'kamandala', and a loincloth that I will render to you.

You must not take part in the social ceremonies or rituals of Kaliyuga-people.

You must not wield or show the wisdom leaves unnecessarily as irrational people will mistake it for some petty ornament, and may conspire to procure it.

You must not use the divine power of the wisdom leaves on others for your own self, unless unavoidable, and with keen judgment.

Anutaapa: Why do I need to protect the wisdom leaves when it is the source of all mystic powers? How can anyone steal them? I am not able to understand, O best of the Brahmin! Please tell.

Sage Paramhamsa: I know, O Anutaapa, for I have asked the same question from my master. These wisdom leaves that you have now are to be secured with utmost intelligence as anyone can take them away from you in a snatch, like a stroke of wind takes away the moisture. And thus you must know that the wisdom leaves cannot be determined by clairvoyance; no yogi can locate them exercising their occult powers, not even in their dreams. You must protect them as a mother protects her child. And if, at any time, you lose them or divest yourself from them, you will be no more than a meek human being, devoid of the acquired extraordinary strength and wisdom! Breathing is what you may stop, but you must not dispossess of them.

Anutaapa: I, if somehow, dispossess these of myself, what danger does it pose? Will the one who finds them procure the powers?

Sage Paramhamsa: The one who finds them, first, must annihilate your material body, and then if he is wise enough, if he is the knower of holy Vedas, may procure some of the powers that were not meant for him; and thus may misuse them for his own material benefit or to pose harm to entire humanity if he wishes. Thus, always remember, you are the sole owner and protector of the wisdom leaves for the next ten thousand years!

Anutaapa: O slayer of ignorance! You have cleared all my doubts. I am ready for my journey.

It was still time until dusk. The '*Panchamruta abhisheka*,' a purification ceremony, must begin before the last sunset of this age. To mark the journey of successor-ship, the disciple must be anointed with the '*Panchamruta*'- a mixture of holy water of the Ganges, honey, cow's fresh milk, ghee, and yoghurt. Anutaapa sat, half-clothed, on a raised platform made of wet sand raked out from the banks. Other disciples started chanting the greatest Vedic hymn.

The hymn meant: The one who rests on the ocean of milk, the great lord! May shower his mercy on the Apaursheya who is abiding by the lord's rule, and beginning his journey. The path is made of thorns, yet he fulfils the lord's desire and accomplishes the duty given to him! May all demi-gods, the sun, the moon, the air, the water, the fire, and others, help him and become the receivers of the Lord's mercy. The Lord prevails! Absolute truth prevails!

Streams of soothing white *Panchamruta* spouted from his forehead like the Ganges from the Himalayas, sanctifying him. Uninterrupted vibrations of the mantra poured into his ears. The auspicious libation continued for an hour; all birds, animals, and trees, and other inhabitants of the forest had fallen asleep under the layer of resonation of the chanting. Anutaapa's skin had developed effulgence with the end of the last hymn, which only meant that the ceremony had been successful. Even a single faulty pronunciation of a single syllable of the Mantra would make the entire ritual a futile effort, leading to unknown effects, and the entire ceremony will have to be carried out once more when the same constellation reappears, which would mean another ten thousand human years.

After bathing in the holy Ganges, Anutaapa was given a *'kamandala'* and a *'loincloth'* which he was going to preserve for the rest of his stay on Earth. "This is your only possession; circumstances will come, good, bad, and worse, but you have only these two with you...and...." Sage Paramhamsa, then, untied a thick swag, the moment that comes after several thousands of years. "...and this..." The Wisdom leaves were now visible to everyone. Paramhamsa presented the swag to Anutaapa; chanting re-started.

Anutaapa stood up and genuflected in front of the master, and embraced the fellow disciples. It was the moment of departure. The master blessed him, and turned towards the river. The memories of childhood that safely resided in his heart under some unknown shadow were appearing uncontrollably around his eyes. Loneliness was what he feared; his lifelong friends were about to retreat, leaving him with a society that he'll never associate with. But he must not entertain the feelings of attachment or separation for long; he was the chosen one. And more than that, this was the repayment, for the imperishable knowledge that the master has blessed his disciple with, and has to be paid in the terms that the master lays. Anutaapa unhesitatingly repaid the debt, without giving up a tear.

Sage Paramhamsa and the six disciples greeted the Ganges and stepped in for the '*Jala-Samadhi*'; the process of voluntarily abandoning one's body by meditating in water and merging with the absolute or super consciousness. The river was as chillingly cold as her origin the Himalayas. The seven dipped themselves deep into the water and never came up. The flowing water had nothing to reveal but the shimmery reflection of the moon, the black trees, and Anutaapa. Night had come alive; animals were now readying themselves for the regular hunt; the remnants of *Panchamruta*, the reminiscent of Sage Paramhamsa's fatherly touch, had been partly absorbed by the sand. Anutaapa lied down, on his knees, near the sandy platform where he was crowned, and stowed the soddened white sand into his *kamandala*. He arose and made for the forests; the last eight hours were indeed unforgettable for him.

Chapter 3

The Diary

When you open this diary, I would have become a palm-full of ashes. So, actually, you would be talking to George Jonathan Stewart's "spirit." I felt that coming, you know... some temporary detachment all of a sudden. That matters! Sometimes it does matter. Matter and spirit!

So, here I am. I don't know how I should begin; never written for others to read. Anyways, hope you are not dull, and would be as good as you had been the last night. I know how different you are from others of your age. I also hope that I have fulfilled all your dreams, you did not have a long list though, and my responsibilities. But If I haven't, if you feel that I haven't...well I have. And If I have, you may read further.

I know you take care of your mother, though you don't like to express it, or don't know how to express it, and there is nothing bad about that, so I need not remind you that you have to take care of her like I had until I became a spirit. I just did remind you. All she has is you, and I have left you everything to make her happy. Of course that includes money, which may or may not make any sense to you. I read that...yours once, a published article, *'the theistic dilemma'*, which concluded after eight paragraphs that– *'Happiness is a relative term, and that very relativity is the cause of unhappiness.'*, but still you will never have to worry about money or earning money.

You haven't forgotten those stories? No, you haven't, those stories of your heroism. *The Backyard Adventures*. Do you recall the day, that day, when you finally stole the backyard room's key? The great key! And you couldn't see your friends for more than a week. You had been a curious kid then, you still are; you would try to coax me into giving up the key every time you caught me strolling around the backyard. You would peep from the window; throw stones in to find if someone's living down there, and that one fine afternoon- when you informed your school teacher about being very rich and your father taming a dinosaur in the backyard, and that she can pay a visit to us. Good old days. I wish I were alive, uh.

As you grew up, you stopped thinking about it, realizing about more significant things in life than hovering over an overestimated backyard, filthy backyard. You were born in London; you came to India, and then went back to London. Never sure of what you will do in your life or with other's life. You have transformed a lot in the last five years. Despite your Indian upbringing, your mother could not dispel you of your atheistic beliefs. This nature of yours has made you miss an interesting aspect, an inseparable aspect of this existence – the Divinity. The very easy to understand fact that the cause of a problem cannot be the solution to the problem. Do you get me? The solution to miseries of this world cannot come out of this world that itself is the cause of all miseries. You get me, right? It's like you are trying to dry yourself while submerged in water.

I am trying hard to sound serious. I am serious.

Alright, I will stop the nonsense. Here is the great key; it's in your right pocket, if you are wearing the same pyjamas, the black ones. It is yours, all yours.

This thing- the controversial basement! It's not a basement actually. I mean it is a graveyard. And no! No! We haven't built a house on a graveyard; it has many graves of our family members, the ancestors, all of your forefathers who came to India, most of them. I have never even counted the number of graves; you are going to go so you can count. So, you know, that is why you can't let a child roam around this collection of graves and force him to lose some sleep. It's quite frightening. I don't know how you would react, but when I first saw the place it had that macabre air sucking you in. Besides, I had been very fond of the horror stories, of late 70s, so I thought I was a little expert on this, but I got very frightened. Wait, I still am, what if any one of them now bumps into me in this ghost world?

Alright, so, this fable has a long history, and it's not one of those haunted mansion series; I shall try to narrate it with a brevity just enough to let you fly above the non-sense zone. So, you can drop all your chores for the day, or, for the night.

You know that, uh, I mean as you have had a prominent part of your schooling here in India, so in your history books you must have read about Sir James Stewart. You have. Turn the pages back to somewhere around the 16th century. It was the time East India Company had established its nine factories in Bengal, trading in cotton, indigo, tea, and other spices. Revenue generation grew by leaps and bounds. And thus the English had started exercising their military power, and permeating the administration too. Many of the merchants were made governors in various states, including Sir James Stewart, who was also the master merchant of two of the nine factories. Fortunately, or unfortunately, this was also the time when the Mughal kingdom was showing the signs of downfall. The local clans of Rajputs, Jats, and many more, I don't know the names of all, had begun their journey to trample the Mughals and gain back their lost wealth. This was a period of highest turbulence, almost indicating an overthrow. And we, the British, were waiting for the right time to usurp as much power as the natives could surrender. Aurangzeb, once a tyrant emperor, was undoubtedly facing the heat from all sides; that's why he had to invite many of the English headmen.

His plans were quite basic- to get maximum support and back-up of the English military with the most urgency and sycophancy. The British governors were bootlicked with enormous servility; the list of presents that they were loaded with was never ending – each governor was given the privilege to pick the most beautiful maiden, male servants to serve them till death, gold ornaments, diamonds, pearls; and, most importantly, they were allowed to set up new factories with heavy tax exemptions. This was the day British had been waiting for-- the chance to seep deep into the roots of the Indian subcontinent. Sir James Stewart explains his experience in the court of Aurangzeb like this:

"I sat there near the throne of the wicked emperor of all times, the Aurangzeb! The courtroom was splendid; I had never seen such an architectural magnificence before; but at the same time it was a stark waste of wealth. The walls were populated with rubies, unnecessarily, and lofty pillars studded with diamonds. Aurangzeb's musnud of gold, structured on a raised platform shrouded with Persian carpets, was surrounded by servants fanning until the court discontinued. He took all his decisions whimsically; the court men had been mere puppets. He unfolded to me a map of his ruled state, and the strength of his men, and described a layman's plan to attack the neighbouring province, which he obviously had conveyed to each of the governors, invited earlier, with the same force. And for this to be successful, he appealed to me for an agreement for military support. I agreed. I couldn't deny the hoard of gold, diamonds, and women, but I had to deceive. The English had a broader dream of ruling the entire subcontinent, uprooting the Mughals first, and Aurangzeb was no more than a pawn to suppress the native and foreign kings. We were to induce him into a false sense of victory. I made clumsy promises, and accumulated the wealth that I couldn't have earned working whole of my life."

Of all the treasure that was showered, there was a wooden box that Aurangzeb himself presented to Sir James Stewart saying he received it from a mystic Hindu saint as a mascot and it had mystic powers; the saint who he had later buried in his Jahgarh fort for unclear reasons.

This wooden box actually had a bunch of metallic plates, which looked golden, sewn together along one edge and wrapped in a silky fabric with Persian verses printed on it. And, very strangely, the plates had extruded surfaces with Sanskrit texts. It had pretence of an amalgamation of Persian and Hindu philosophies.

Aurangzeb's reign soon ended, he died a mysterious death, and this became the reason for Sir James Stewart's acute attraction towards that bunch of plates. Was it really such a mascot with so much field of influence on the emperor that he lost all his kingdom and life soon after his separation from it?

Nobody knew what it did but Sir James Stewart felt it to be welcoming; so much so that he gave up his position and retired. Indian mysticism bewilders one, and, obviously, he had fallen prey to it on the day he landed. He went into a state of solitary confinement for years to study Sanskrit and Persian - He would wake up before sunrise to practice, and recite, the Sanskrit hymns with a very learned Sanskrit scholar whom he was paying a gold coin a day, and in the noon would learn Persian.

His friends, who visited him during those days, although he had stopped entertaining them, described his enthusiasm towards that metallic book. I would now onwards refer to it as a book, that's what it really is. So, his friends described his enthusiasm similar to that of an Indian elephant invading a sugarcane field. He had grown his beard, had uncut hair, and didn't bathe for days. This devoted learning of the languages only resulted in a conclusion that the silky shroud with Persian prints and the metallic book with Sanskrit prints had nothing in common and one of them was out of place, and it was the former one. When he translated one of the extruded texts, it said: "I, Apaursheya, the blessed, pray to the supreme power to deliver this human of all the sufferings, and give him peace, and all his needs are fulfilled! May the truth and religiousness prevail!"

You may wonder how I could know what he translated some centuries ago with such precision;

every word written here had been descending as it is in our lineage, like the metallic book itself.

However, he couldn't translate many of them; neither could he tell his teacher to translate; it was his secret voyage to mysticism. He fancied he could procure some powers by reciting those texts during the sacred months of the Hindu calendar. His wife would have divorced him had he not suffered a paralysis attack -just what happened to me, and he then left the research. Most of his organs stopped functioning; he lost his eyesight, but his flair for the book never ended. He persuaded his son, Michael Stewart, to drive this research cart. I don't have an explanation for this but Michael Stewart too passed away at an early age. It is not that the mascot had turned into a curse, but perhaps it was no less than that. I am also not saying that our family has been suffering from this curse and I want you to liberate us from it; 'us' would exclude me. But I urge you to do something about it. I want you to dispose of this box in any way you can, so it doesn't become a trouble for you or for someone who finds this box after you, in case you have plans to abandon this house and relocate.

So, have I ever ventured into this? No, I haven't. I wasn't brave enough. In fact, I did not have any reason to venture into this. My father did not want me to do this. Moreover, I have had what I had ever desired; money, fame, a good wife, and an obedient son.

Why would I want to push my son for this? Your vision of life, and this nature, and this world, is contrastingly different from others; you are ahead of your age.

You travel in buses only to find pick-pockets to have a conversation with them. You wear threadbare shirts to see people's reaction to it. You are a millionaire; you can buy any darned thing. But been living this ignorant life just to feed the heavy appetite of the curious mind of yours, and nobody has ever told you to do so. And I couldn't stop you. You are a free runner.

You know yourself more than me.

That's all I had to say. You would have understood the urgency? Now, you can, unlock it, and see to it. And because it's not a household-cleaning job, I advise you to have a closer look at it, and find the depth. Where has all this come from? Who put this bizarre stuff here? Whom does it belong to? Just find that one-eyed owner who untied this beast from the peg?

Do not ever discuss it with anyone who you think might help you. Because it may ultimately land at a museum in a glass-box, yes it's not a far-fetched idea, after being titled as some antique piece of art. That may lead to more accidents. I fear piles of dead men. Because whoever had this was attracted to its magnificence so strongly that he left all his worldly affairs and was made to suffer.

Pursue this day in, day out. You will win over it. You can solve the greatest of mysteries. Trust yourself; atheists are more tactful anyways.

Atheism is an impatient seed of theism waiting for the first rains.

It is your duty.

Have a great day.

Best of luck, or as you have been saying, best of chances!

Chapter 4

A nutaapa continued to re-establish the principles of religiousness, and liberated people from miseries for hundreds of years as he was commanded to do. He would disguise himself in various forms of animals, at times a woman or a child; his real identity was guessed by many but revealed to only a few knowers of Vedas, who had learned about the successors present on the planet Earth to protect the Dharma.

3000 BC, Anutaapa's age was numerically more than four thousand years but the radiance on his forehead was that of a yogi in his twenties. Once a week, he would eat dry leaves, buds, or sometimes a ripe fruit, thus minimizing the excrement processes; the energy needed to run his vital organs was extracted from air in the form of breath by practicing *pranayama* and other forms of yoga. He nestled in the Sundarban forests of eastern parts of ancient India (today's Bangladesh); this had been the longest stay, at one place, of his nomadic life that demanded seclusion from society of Kaliyuga people; but his departure letter was soon delivered.

A severe drought loomed over Laikhat village of today's Rajasthan, hemmed in on all sides by desert. The major population of this village was that of 'Vaishyas' who did trading and agriculture, with one family of 'Shudras' living on the outskirts of Laikhat. Rising temperature was taking its toll on cattle and equally on humans. There was no harvest this year and last year's grain stocks were mere dregs.

People, starved and parched, were abandoning their burdensome cattle, leaving them under open skies, inscribing blood marks on their skin using pointed goads, in a blind-faith of being seen by Rain-God, who may, out of compassion, shower the village; not even their carcasses received a drop of water. Most of the ponds had dried and some other ponds of far-flung villages only showcased muddy water. Many wild animals that came near the pond in search of water were beaten and killed to satisfy the needs of many hungry stomachs. The daytime activity had nearly stopped; the village had the stillness of a burial ground when the sun was on. Scorching sunlight dissected the earth to suck out every sign of life.

The banyan tree, under which had assembled the headmen to address the village once a week, under which had played the children with their carts, under which had sat the talkative women on unoccupied evenings, under which had dawdled the buffaloes, was now a powdery skeleton.

The daily chores had to be done in the nights so as to cause the least perspiration and uneasiness. Male members of the family would visit the neighbouring villages with earthen pots one over the other, to procure water from their open reservoirs. Most of the collected water was consumed on the way as men had to cover the distance by foot, and the leftover was offered to the family. This practice, too, soon came into notice by the competitors and had to be stopped, making their lives drier.

Anutaapa held the wisdom leaves in his hand, chanted a mantra, and with his power of clairvoyance came to know about the miserable circumstances the Laikhat village was in; after contemplating the past and present karmas of each creature that moved on the land circumscribed he transferred his body with the speed of mind and sat under the banyan tree. He had now disguised himself in the form of a hundred year old Sadhu; bearing Vishnu marks on his body and a floating beard, he draped himself in torn saffron clothes. He opened his sunken eyes and started observing the passers-by in the dark; men had already departed, and only women were to be seen who were on the look-out for dry wood to ignite fire in the kitchen- the food was an illusion as it had been no more than a boiled mixture of roots or leaves. Malnourished children slept for most of the day inside; their bodies were meatless and so frail that they couldn't even stand themselves on their feet. Amidst this dismal state he remained like a statue under the banyan for two days. Three men had died, soon after his arrival, left to decompose on open lands due to the dire scarcity of ceremonial resources. After a week, a few women took notice of him; not him but his "ominousness."

Anutaapa could hear the faintest of whispers.

"Have you seen that old man sitting near the banyan?"

"...and his sinister eyes? His presence has doomed our village, and many have died..."

"...you are very right, however dire this draught is but no one had died till now...we must unite and call the headmen..."

"...why call the headmen? We better ask him to leave right now."

Women approached the Sadhu sitting under the banyan that itself sat bare under the moon.

"O old man! Open your eyes! You have been sitting here for a week; why have you come here?"

The Sadhu instantly replied, without meeting their eyes, "What harm am I doing to you sitting here? This banyan tree is my old friend. I have come to meet him. I am going to stay here forever!"

"Forever? Your body is withering, you will soon die of the thirst and hunger, and no one is going to feed you! Leave from here!" He didn't bother to reply and let the moments of whispers pass.

Next morning, a man who was returning from the water-voyage, and whose house had been the only one near the banyan, called his wife out and shouted, as he had been hard of hearing, "O Mahatma! O Mahatma! Laikhat is facing a dreadful drought; don't expect any alms! You must take refuge in some other village as soon as possible! Wake up! And go!" No word was heard from the Sadhu.

"This Sadhu is sitting here for the past eight days, in harsh sunlight and without food or water; he doesn't even sweat! Look at him..." The man told several others who came along with him, "I can't stand the burning earth beneath my feet; let's go in..."

Anutaapa spoke in a stern voice, "This village is sinful! Every man here is sinful! And his wife and children must suffer and partake of their share of penance! Beware! This most selfish crowd of men!"

"You, yourself, are about to die! Impostor! By your spell of black magic you have killed our men! And this evening, we will make you leave from here!"

"Who are you, asking me to leave? You all are not only clutched by this calamity, but also by ego, greed, and selfishness! Your mind has become your own enemy! This drought will extract life out of everyone, and you are not going to receive any rainfall, not a drop, in the coming years! Clan of fools! You all will die!"

"Such an audacity! Let's call the headman at the vision of dusk and banish him!"

The gathering had dwindled away, succumbing to scalding winds to which Anutaapa had been insensitive. As the sun descended, the sensation of life had lulled itself but the astonishing news of an impostor Sadhu under a banyan had circulated all over; this provided a sense of false relief as they kept mouthing off about him rather than brooding over the drought.

The headman was waiting anxiously for the dusk to come, and soon it came and saw the gathering of villagers, around the banyan, who were referring to Anutaapa as "sadhu sitting under banyan." Thus, the name "banyan" was being called more often, which made the tree feel more accompanied. The loud man who had been hard of hearing cued the headman, who was half the age of Anutaapa, to speak. The turban bearing man scrutinised the Sadhu with plain surprise, and so did his young son who murmured impatiently.

"O old man! Dressed in saffron, tell us who you are? I am the headman of Laikhat village, the administrator of all trade and the in-charge security of villagers. Answer me!"

"Who appointed you the headman? For you can't save your men from dying! How could you, when you are yourself a fool!" Anutaapa retorted sharply.

"Don't deride our misery, old man!" the headman's son barged in. "It is the Rain-god to whom we wish to offer our sacrifices and not an impostor!"

"No doubt you have displeased the Rain-god, and displeased your fortune!" Anutaapa eyed the sky. Hearing about the displeasure of the Rain-god, the crowd sitting on the dust became anxious and the headman seated himself next to Anutaapa, with folded hands, asking, "My son is furious over this year's losses, pardon him! We do not expect any sages visiting us these days and thus the villagers considered you ominous. Please tell us how we could rescue our lives!"

"If you offer me your most valuable possession, this night, I will exchange water for it. I will give water weighing a hundred times of it only to one who offers me his most valuable possession! And there is no other way." This was so unbelievable to some of them that they now considered him a dacoit and hailed obscenities at him.

"A Sadhu never accumulates valuables! This is a dacoit who has plans to deceive us! Beat him to death! And feed his body to vultures!"

"He is an illusionist from hell! By now we would have crossed half of the distance towards the pond!"

While others, who had been passionate merchants in their good days, began making the calculations and thinking of the heaviest possible thing they owned. "Will you accept cow dung cakes?" The crowd was now at its feet, some decided to leave the place considering it wastage of precious night-time, and some went closer to the banyan and speculated on him as if they could discover how he was going to manifest water out of nowhere.

The children, who had until now been sitting silent and had understood nothing, were amazed to learn that the stars and the moon had been appearing in the night the same way as before despite the monstrous drought.

The headman meddled in, "Those who have not found the offer worthy may leave, and the rest, at their whims, can wager. I will, myself, bring my most valuable possession!"

The last statement of the headman made a constructive impact and many people foraged their homes for things that would win them the water deal. Not more than eight hours were available, and the mental and physical strain that the ordeal demanded from their weak bodies, shrank the span of that night.

With a miscellany of "valuables" and people pouring in, a fair had surfaced near the venue when midnight had passed; reminiscent of the fair that used to be held near the Okhra pond, once every three months, when Laikhat's Vaishyas traded their goods for camels and goats.

"What have you to offer?" Anutaapa asked an eagerly waiting man.

"I have brought two buffalo; they are not producing milk but they used to, and I had purchased them for five goats!"

"Go away! Selfish! And awaken your dormant soul!"

Another man came in pushing everyone. "I have these huge camels; look at them! Such a drought and they are still standing, more powerful than these lame buffaloes! What do you say? Can you get a better barter than this?"

"Go away! Selfish! And awaken your dormant soul!"

A woman who considered herself wiser than any other in the village tried to bargain with flattery. "You are a great saint who has been incarnated to save us from the furious Rain-God, the knower of everything, more kind than any demi-god of heavens; please accept my bronze anklets! They are most valuable to me!"

"Go away! Selfish! And awaken your dormant soul!"

Then came a sweating potter humping a sack on his spine. "These are all selfish, O Mahatma! I give to you the earthen vessels that I made, last year, with my hands working day and night; I am the most hard-working!"

"Go away! Selfish! And awaken your dormant soul!"

It took them by surprise that they had made a countless number of offerings and each had been disapproved with the same disgust. Every newcomer was not a villager but a deja-vu to the rejected ones who stood aloof discussing in their minds- what had gone wrong? Which "soul" is being talked about, why is it dormant and, above all, what has it in common with the water-deal?

The headman had watched all this happen, and he shortly concluded to his son, "Indeed they are foolish; they do not even know the meaning of valuables, son! If we get the water weighing a hundred times more than golden brick, we'll have much surplus water to sell and that'll even compensate for the loss of this brick one day!"

"Is anyone left?" he made a quick announcement overwhelmed about his decision to choose one of the bricks he had stowed in the safe.

"Is there anyone left who is yet to make an offer?" The villagers knew quite certainly that the headman was the richest of all, and that was why he was chosen the "headman," and he would lay his cards in the end to show his potency and astonish the Sadhu.

"I know that they have all disappointed you; pardon them! I now lay before you my most valuable possession - this golden brick! It took me my life to earn this. Kindly accept this and bless me!" The brick had shone in all directions, illuminating the hands in which was it held, and seemed as a frozen driblet of moonshine that had fallen on Earth.

"Go away! Selfish! And awaken your dormant soul!" Anutaapa threw his fingers at him with a force that declared the awful end of this adventure. Not a word was said or thought and there was no sound but whistling of the wind. The fair did not want to disintegrate before accosting the Sadhu.

The headman's answerability to the villagers was on a par with Anutaapa and he came back strongly. "What are you trying to do? No one has gone to the pond because of you, in the hope that one of us would get enough water for coming days. I have awarded you the respect of a saint and, if you don't have an answer, I will not hesitate to leave you at their hands!"

Anutaapa ignored the warning and stood up. "Is there any who is sinless left in Laikhat village to come and give to me his most valuable possession?"

A wrinkled man burdening himself on his curvy walking stick was seen moving forwards towards the accumulation. He walked like an underdeveloped human owing to the shape of his legs, which had been of similar curvature as the stick.

"Who has invited him?" The headman's son said ostentatiously as the old man was nearing. He raised his stooping head to see the strength of the fair, only to feel out of place, for he neither had anything in his hands, nor had he been carrying on his back a thing that could attract eyes.

"Why doesn't he die? I can't stand the ugly sight of him! ...and he has come here when he himself is a beggar!" He was too broken to answer, and his toothless face had more lines of despair, and denial, than the lonely banyan. The small distance between him and the Sadhu was no less than an ocean where he was trying to row his boat against the waves of old-age, and, the boat being holed by the villagers with the sword of spite, humiliating him from tip to toe.

"Come fast! Shudra! Can't even walk properly! His greed has dragged him to here. Greed doesn't let you live peacefully. Fast! God is not going to give you more legs!" The headman's young son laughed scornfully with everyone, breaking the silence, and only two stayed wordless- Anutaapa and the old man himself. As he reached the Sadhu, the crowd shrunk back; not, obviously, as a gesture of respect for the old man but because he was reeking of decomposing flesh. The cloth, that could only cover his genitals, had frayed to invisibility.

"Accept my obeisance, great sage!" He further bowed down with his folded hands.

"Come and sit here; you cannot walk..." Anutaapa accepted his obeisance. "What have you brought? Do not fear them! Reveal your possession!" The old man didn't sit down.

"I am a Shudra. I have no right to sit beside a Brahmin...and I am a beggar..." The old man, hanging himself on the inseparable stick, unfolded his right fist. "I live in a hut at the outskirts of Laikhat; I have nothing with me to be called a possession except a stone that I grinded to make a small vessel. I am ignorant, and a committer of sins. I only have these last drops of water to offer you, for I could not have come to visit a Brahmin empty-handed. I have no strength to walk to the pond; I am praying each day for my death...I do not have anything except this, O great sage, and I do not beg water in return but a peaceful death, which only a sage can endow! This is my last begging...liberate me. Liberate me..." He coughed as many times as he asked of liberation. Anutaapa gently held his shivering palm, and drank the moisture with the contentment of an end he had been waiting for.

"You have accumulated a good quantity of water in your homes, each one of you! In this drought, there is water, and only water, that is your most valuable possession. If you did not consider water the most valuable, then, why did you want water in exchange for gold, or ornaments or animals! You are deceiving your own soul! This old man, who is dying every day, who has no one to feed him in this withered stage of life, who is bearing the pain of bereavement because one of you had murdered his family members! Who cannot walk to the pond and has been begging water at every threshold, and who is denied water at every threshold, offers me his drops of water." Villagers now, unknowingly, started speculating that since he knew the past and present of this Shudra, he may be one of those highly mystic saints from the Himalayas. "You have eagerly, and purposely, sinned, each one of you!"

"This argument is unjust. How can we offer our water to this Shudra when we have, at our home, thirsty children? Why should we give up our family, and ourselves, and instead save his life? Helping someone is indeed going to give one heaven, but if we don't have sufficient means to help others, will we be called sinners? This is unjust!" The headman's young son replied passionately.

"He is the only beggar of the village! Even a drop from every doorstep could make his living. Why you do not offer him anything is because he is a Shudra! Accept the truth, and nothing will be unjust!"

"How can we ridicule Vedas, for they say a Shudra cannot enter the house of a Vaishya, because he is born sinner? He will pollute our minds, and make us born as a Shudra in our next birth!"

"O false proclaimer of Vedas! Do not make your concoctions about the Vedic-religion! That is by far the greatest sin! A man is never *born* a Shudra, or a Vaishya, or a Brahmin, or a Kshatriya. The division of society that Vedas pronounce is strictly based on your actions. A Brahmin's son who doesn't understand Vedic wisdom, or doesn't want to learn it sincerely, without saying becomes a Shudra! And a Shudra's son, who aspires to learn Vedic principles, and preach God's message, undoubtedly belongs to the class of highly elevated Brahmins! And a fool like you devises his own notions, and follows and propagates them till death; and thus the religiousness is severely dampened to give birth to thousands of sinners, and the society suffers from natural calamities like this!" Anutaapa's voice gradually increased to put the headman's son, and every other villager, in a state of armless defence. "...and those! Those of you, who boast of being merciful to this old man, remember it is not you but it is his forgiveness that will allow you still to get water to drink! Fifty years ago, when he was a young man, and could plough, your fathers ate the very grains of this Shudra's field, the cattle of theirs grazed unrestrictedly, and every drop of sweat went unpaid, and is still unpaid! You and your coming generations would repay the debt with the same usuries as you charge in your trading! You would repay! Or will suffer natural calamities, one after another, and another!"

The sermon delivered under the banyan cleansed the mouldy hearts, for the words came out of the successor of the world himself, and the headman with his son genuflected before the Sadhu and the old man, and begged, not for water, but for clemency until they heard him again, "If you repay the debt, you, along with your families will flourish again," Anutaapa declared.

"As you say! The omniscient!" The headman could not think of anything else, as he had closed his eyes in a state of numbness.

"Where he lives," Anutaapa finger-tipped his wisdom leaves covertly, and nodded, "that small hut! In front of it you will find a large pond, which is bottomless, brimming with fresh water that will never go dry! It can satiate the desires of hundreds of villages. There, you will bow down before him to fill your vessels, and pay him an amount of your earned grains as much as you desire but as many times as you fill! "

"...and you have to live twenty more years, and preach them all you have learned, and then die peacefully," he told the old man.

Laikhat village, today, is more commonly known as 'Laiht' in its degenerated form. The bottomless pond exists to date as Anutaapa predicted but there is no hut left or the "old man." The only witness left is the banyan tree which still exists, exuberant, and a temple which encompasses it. An idol of an unnamed Sadhu, worshipped by the localities, is said to fulfil every wish. This true story of Anutaapa or the "Apaursheya" is alive, and is recited, in the form of many assorted fables, in the villages of Rajasthan.

Chapter 5

The backyard room was not an anonymous place; it was there since the Stewarts had it erected. Unfrequented and homesick in hometown, like a widower, it was missing human presence and care; the care which could have garnished its beauty and the human presence that would have made it feel a part of this mansion, and not the idle appendix. Audin had been here several times but that was long ago, and the door was always found locked, when he was a notorious child of twelve. The room never saw the kid after that, and it wasn't aware that Audin was alive and had been growing up happily. When Audin last came here it was his voluntary attempt to cut the two feet of long grass, though he didn't know much about a lawn mower. The room appeared to have a low ceiling nearly equal to Audin's height, just about five feet eleven inches; this gave an impression that it had caved in over years, or were the dead trying to drag it down to the core of the earth?

Surrounding the room was land, once a garden, now strewn with all varieties of scrap. Plastic buckets, iron rods, ropes, fused bulbs, drain pipes, and other nameless objects of only human interest picketed the room from all sides. The flower pots, which once embellished the roof, were no more beautiful than evil-eye wanderers. From the roof hung a choked drain pipe whose fixtures needed immediate fixing; it couldn't drain even air but was an affectionate shelter of blind crickets.

The walls never got white-washed after they were planted; they had gone dry, severely, as if Mr Stewart got them stolen from a sand dune of the Thar.

Rama evasively disagreed to accompany him to the backyard, and then agreed evasively.

The evening was usual, just another ending of one of the days of a year; Audin peeped in from a small crevice on the side wall but couldn't distinguish anything from the dark. Another blind cricket!

"Do you see something?" Rama whispered.

"Why are you whispering? We are not trespassing on somebody else's property."

"We would awaken a ghost." Rama spoke tersely, almost in compulsion.

"You know about these ghosts?" Audin was still peeping unflinchingly so as to let Rama change his opinion.

"Any ghost can enter a human through their body hair; one must not fool around with graves after dark."

"All of them are my forefathers. They know me, perhaps."

"You must recite the Vedic Hymns before entering, or don't enter at all."

"They were all Christians, I guess, before being dead. Would they even understand the 'Vedic' hymns?"

Rama never wanted to go in; he had read in his scriptures about ghosts being most active after sunset, and that they often like to "come out" of their bedding as soon as the living clowns of the mad world put a halt at their mockery. Audin dragged aside the scrap heaps and made the way. Worn out tyres which ran on the most expensive cars had accumulated water and were lying helplessly as unwanted responsibilities.

"I still don't believe this to be a part of your house. It's a breeding station of these insects. Let's move out of here!"

"None of this is mine...been deliberately put in here to stop anyone from going inside...a kind of a fence..."

Rama felt the nauseating smell travelling up his nose that pleaded him to run away like one of the agile ghosts of this evening but he couldn't; Audin had always been there for him through thick and thin.

Seventeen years ago, a day before Diwali, Rama, who was in seventh grade then, puckered his face, clinching to his father's arm, as they both stood watching their small house razed by government goons. The house which was brick-layed by his father himself got uprooted in one light-hearted stroke of the steel jaws of bulldozer. A farmer is like a free but poor artist who sketches the field with his plough and whose entire living depends on somebody else's will- the rains or the rain god; the only treasure he has is a promising piece of land. Rama's father spent his entire youth transforming the hut into a cemented house; bit by bit he would raise the walls a foot a day, dreaming of a secure future for his family which now appeared like a stress mark on the word *gloom*.

The expropriation was being justified by a crumbled sheet of official paper with a seal and signatures which his father couldn't understand.

"This is my land...Go away...You have no right to touch it... Please go away!" Rama's father was fighting a rear-guard action.

"Who says it's not your land, Harish Chandra? It has always belonged to you and that's why we are offering you this money." A policeman cornered Rama's father. "Would you sign this...?"

Rama's house was built on the outskirts of Delhi in an area which had recently become the latest business centre of fatty builders. They said the "mall" was a gift to the village and a sign of development and prosperity, for which Harish Chandra could become a hero by making this simple sacrifice. The highway on which the mall was to be built scythed straight through Rama's fields, thus their small house hampered "development" and "prosperity."

"Where would I go without my fields? This money is not enough to buy even one month's grains! Have mercy on us! I beg you!"

"Look Harish, we can't cheat government, we are honest people, and we are paying as per the prices they have fixed for everyone. Go to the city; do some work with your wife and children; there are enough requirements of labourers. I know a man who runs many iron moulding factories. You will definitely get some work there."

Rama couldn't bear the sight of everything being smoothened; he broke into tears and his father had no reason to console him.

"We have always been labourers, my son; do not worry; we will be doing good in the city and I will not let you become a poor labourer like me. You will keep going to the same school..."

The school was expensive where riches like George Jonathan Stewart sent their children. Working ten hours a day in the factory fetched Harish Chandra six thousand rupees a month and the school fees had nearly been the same; the money that he accumulated from last year's harvest was paid in setting up a shack in a slum colony. Rama soon, obviously, left the school as it was a one sided game between bread and books, and was admitted to a neglected government school that ran in evenings.

Audin finally took notice, after two days, that his close friend had been absent from the class. This had never happened before. Audin did not want to misunderstand anything and asked one of the drivers at the Nirvana to drop him to his special friend's place on the same day.

"I knew he lived here...in these fields." Audin was confused to look at the huge building under construction, as if he had missed a hundred chapters of a long narrative.

"There is no house here, Audin. There is construction all around..."

They would never have sold their land. Would I ever be able to see Rama again?

"Can you ask that man in white clothes?" Audin pointed to the man commanding the masons.

"As you say...but there will be no use..."

"But it will lead us to a state better than we are in now."

"Oh! That farmer! Harish Chandra! He has left from here...I had known him for years..."The man spoke very loudly trying to overcome the sound of cement mixers. Audin came out of the car as soon as he heard the name. "Vijay Pratap Singh ji has bought this land from him. He couldn't resist the amount of money and left for the city; he lives there only."

"In the city? Where in the city?" Audin interrupted, as if infected with joy by that man's last statement.

"How would I know? But Vijay Pratap Singh ji is so kind that he also offered him a job in the Stewarts' iron mills. He is such a man of honour."

Almost as a reflex action, the next stop for the driver was the mill and Mr Stewart was not informed about his son's emergency visit. Audin, very poised like a client in a tight-fit fancy dress, was sitting in the plush cabin of his father's.

"You have never been to this place before? Have you?" Mr Stewart was amused to detect the faint line of interest of his son in his father's business.

"Do you know about Rama? His house was razed by someone who had such a long name that I don't remember, I don't want to remember, and he was forced to work in this mill. They would never sell their land for money, and he is still working here; I don't find this good. Is it good? I fear Rama has left the school too."

"Rama's father?"

Audin couldn't speak a word to Rama when he sat next to him once again on the same bench, in the same class. "Why are you not speaking to me?" Rama poked Audin.

"I am sorry. I feel bad about it."

"No, you have saved my life, my family's life. Had your father not set up this work, we would have died of hunger, and it is because of you that I am able to step in this school again. My mother says that you will be a great man one day... "

"I don't remember my mother saying that to me anytime. What does she say about you?"

"She says that I must do whatever you ask me to..."

"If I ask you to share your lunch? And this sweater?"

Rama's father was escalated to a superior role, and he was not a labourer anymore. Though Mr Stewart presented him with a farmhouse to live in, a car, and the post of supervisor, Harish Chandra only chose one and said, "Your debt will remain a debt, Mr Stewart, but I promise to serve you, with my family, until I die...”

Rama rolled down his sleeves to disguise mosquitoes and cupped his mouth with an already humid handkerchief. They were standing in front of an overweight wooden door, a double door, much heavier for the standard use. Its antique wood had turned darker, the last shade before one becomes pitch black, and dull and appeared like the bark of an old witch-crafted tree. The hand-carved images of a Hindu goddess were not easily recognizable because of the chips that had started peeling off - a woman sitting on a tarred lotus surrounded by leaves and playing a sitar had become headless. A twin of hers, of the same excellence, had been present on the adjacent half.

“It has the same door as your room... ”

The two ladies supported a mammoth lock that gave the impression of a dead-end, but the six-inched key was as sharp and fierce as an arrow. Audin lifted the lock to slide in the oiled key.

“It has unlocked!” Rama filtered his voice out of the handkerchief as the lock fell open at once by the mere shadow of the key, though he was dead sure that it wouldn’t.

Any lock this old doesn’t abide by the rules of a key.

“Someone has been using the keys very often. Who else but my father?” Audin pushed the door in. It didn't move beyond two inches dragging heavily against the floor like a retired wrestler devoid of any strength but not his will to fight back. The frame supporting the door was covered with moth-holes and dried larvae in an unknown language, as if they – the moths and the larvae, had been mindless architects.

Rama forbade himself from touching it. "We can call somebody else to open it?"

"No, it will open if you help me push it!" Audin's face was gushing with redness.

Rama scanned the door panel for the cleanest surface to butt. A scrunch! And Audin tumbled down on the broad footsteps beneath the door. The ground was three feet deep, and accordingly the ceiling seemed suitably high.

"Watch it!" Rama didn't come down. He had frosted over. With some slurry of sediments, and a stay of few more years in this position and character- twisted fingers clung to the door handle, feet zigzagging on the upper most step, he would have transformed himself into a new species of archaeopteryx.

"Let's leave; there is no oxygen inside!"

"The moisture content is quite high; come down. It is not that deep; there is enough oxygen." Audin stood up, panting.

"But I should wait here, and keep a watch that nobody comes in."

"I can't see you, where have you gone?"

"Can you throw me some light with your cell-phone? Give it to me. Mine is with him, he would have fired it by now." The cell-phone's torch passed a white stream of light that created a geometric pattern out of nowhere. Audin lowered himself to find where he had been standing. He was suppressing a grass turf of a mound.

It was a grave.

"Audin...Audin you are on a grave..." Rama pointed pushing his eyeballs out.

"Aren't they dead? And free of guilt, envy, pride, and everything you describe as sin; why would you fear then."

"They are not. They have all kinds of desires, and are always on a look-out to satisfy them. Rishi ji told me once. You better get out of here. We are in a very inauspicious place!"

He reflected the stream of light towards the ceiling to invent a mental picture of the room in this "blindness". Rama held himself more tightly in a secured position to run away any moment. A brown, hemispherical, porcelain switch was found fixed adjacent to the door. He lifted it up, and a bulb enveloped in webs flickered and for a moment the room was a small movie theatre.

"It is the first bulb Edison invented, with age old electric wiring." The architecture of the room matched the rest of the Nirvana mansion. As was with every other room, this too had two feet deep niches meant for placing statues in the front walls, but statues had been absent. The accumulated dust layers seemed pieces of abstract art by the winds. The room was bigger in size then it had appeared from outside.

A cat sprawling in the driest corner growled; reminding the foreigners of the offence of lightening the bulb, and growled again to warn not to stare at her new born kittens.

"This is a black cat." Rama was sure of the bad omen that had just been encountered, but Audin's confident posture stifled his direct thoughts. Cats have been chosen almost unanimously to represent misfortune and evil, but the one dwelling here with her family appeared less harmless and more social. She kept talking in her growl since the beginning of the face-off, like an extrovert.

"There is no unusual feeling about this room; that is how a secluded room should be; what do you say?"

"You hear the cat? It symbolizes deception, hypocrisy. That's a bad omen. Somebody is trying to stop us here! That's not usual!"

"It is the beauty of this nature; beneath the soil lies the dead and above is the budding life; how is she even eligible for being a bad omen? They don't even demand comforts to reproduce, unlike us." Audin appreciated the processes of nature, particularly the animalistic ones, more than Rama appreciated God. He often supported the idea that human "opposition" to God or his "collaboration" with God doesn't make any difference to either party; the processes of nature propagate without needing any divine intervention, thus judging such processes as bad or good omens is carelessness only.

"I have never seen any animal committing a sin-from your list of sins. They don't. They can't. But a human can, of course from your list of sins, and when a human does, he is upfront compared to animals. Isn't that so hypocritical of us?" Audin was least aware that this was not at a decorated polemic stage where he had been invited to only argue; it was a graveyard, where they have come to exhume from one of the graves all the paraphernalia that Mr Stewart mentioned in his diary.

"Oh! Young saviour of cats! Look! The sun has already set, and if you just want to chit chat about your fancy dogmas, I will be more than happy to go and find a deaf listener for you! Why can't you just be quick?"

The bulb glowed more fluorescently as the night started to make her presence felt. The names written on the dwarf headstones appeared more legible. The graves were many and were scattered around all over like history books fallen off a shelf.

Sir James Stewart (1680-1732)
Michael Stewart (1712-1742)
Crook Stewart (1737-1757)
...

...

Mark Stewart (1778-1798)

If there had been no mentioning of the dates, it could have been concluded that all of them died together in a family function.

Audin took off his shoes and squatted down near Mark's grave; it was the latest, just about two hundred years old; and started to burrow with his hands like a shabby school child. As we grow up, as we have to, we stop climbing rooftops, and smearing walls, and teasing stray dogs, and jumping unclothed, and talking gibberish, and digging soil; an expression of our agreement to the social norms of pleasure for an adult. Audin, however, didn't pay heed to any of such self-explanatory norms; his fingernails were now packed with grassy soil. Rama threw the shovel in; he wasn't yet ready to deplane the flight of three steps, and shouted, "We are going to be late. I will not be able to stay here after nine."

"I am digging very hard, and this shovel may wake someone down there who you are afraid of." Audin was already sweating.

"I will not stay here after nine!" Rama reassured that no question be raised afterwards if he disowns his dear friend when the clock strikes nine.

"But you will miss this peace. The calm that a graveyard has is nowhere else to be found. Maybe that's why people like to rest here when they die." Audin was not even looking at Rama's face; Rama, on the other hand, had not taken his eyes off the cell-phone for the last ten minutes.

Meanwhile, the cat picked up her kittens with her mouth to transport them to a safer place where there would be no sharp moving objects and noise. As if she knew the intruders were planning to work here past their sleeping time. She showed her concerns by occasional moaning (or singing as Audin perceived); with every single moan Rama felt his life span shortening by the pace of a sand clock. And felt that including the cat, and her kittens, all the men from underneath are looking at him in a very crooked way; that he must be ready for the vengeance whenever the right time comes as he is the sole accused for this unholy act.

"I think I have disturbed the kittens; I had to. I am here for the first time; they will grant pardon. It is called the debutant's benefit." Audin's apology to the animals perhaps went unnoticed. To extend Rama's waiting spree, there was no halt to digging as there were no signs of either a bone that had lost its muscular covering or something that resembled a box.

Maybe the bones got decomposed. But the box?

The tensed silence broke; the cell-phone rang at the loudest sound level and fell out of his hands. He didn't pick it, and it kept ringing, for his one hand was busy gripping the door handle and the other was trying to lengthen itself to reach the ground. A devotional rhyme played repeatedly and the screen flashed his wife's name in capitals.

"Your phone? Rama?"

"It's her."

Audin stopped his shovel for a second to relish his countenance. Rama picked up the phone, concentrating with the precision of a shooter and the elasticity of an acrobat.

I dare not touch any part of my body to the burial ground.

"I am here! Here with Audin." He was the most truthful in answering her calls, "Yes, I will."

"Yes. Yes..." She hung up.

The trench had now been four feet deep and the pile of extracted soil was already aiming high.

"Shall we leave? If we can continue this on Sunday? The day after tomorrow?" Rama asked in a settled voice. Outside, the frogs had started croaking and were re-surfacing for dinner all together, maybe because of the feeble rain. The humidity levels were pumping up and the giant bulb effused more heat than ever. Audin took off his shirt coloured in sweat; Rama was coloured in restlessness. Audin was a regular jogger at the Ridge, but working like a miner was putting out his heat engines. Eventually his tiredness outlived his will. The frequency of shovel strokes was decreasing and with each stroke the force dampened.

Should I come again on Sunday? Alright, then, let's call it off.

"Come up! You've been toiling in the mood of an ass. Hold back." Rama knew, it was obvious and necessary for him to know of this matter, that his make-no-contribution policy for the aforesaid activity of a forgetful undertaker, was going to be considered treacherous if Audin didn't mind calling it that; still he had found it reasonable to not manoeuvre the principle of not disinterring a grave; it was so *sinful*, or may be, in his balanced mind, being treacherous was less *sinful*.

The wild shovel had frozen in the ground, and resisted Audin's pulling it out, as if it had suddenly remembered to do something which it was to have done a year before. It had stuck in the "something" the duo expected to be a box, and for a while void thoughts prevailed all over the air. Audin unearthed the "something;" with the shovel still in it he brought it out of the room like a memento. The two men had much to say but no words could survive the journey from the wind pipe to the tongue- such moments of surprise have happened many times before in the world's history - imagine an early Babylonian astrologer who got told in his sleep that earth was round!

"We have it."

"Yes...we have it."

Audin had begun dusting the box, and plucking away the weeds. Rama now was in less of a hurry to leave, he was calm, and looked downwards with a desire. The box, or its presence rather, had poured a couple of glassfuls of fresh juice to the men on this laborious evening. For Rama- he found himself one step closer to substantiating his theistic claims and prove to Audin the existence of the supernatural. For Audin- he found himself one step closer to ridiculing

Rama's claims and proving this a mere artwork of a buried civilization, which had been wandering from generations to generations aimlessly.

"Diamonds." The box was generously studded with diamonds that reflected every speck of light, coming out of the room, hundreds of times, to dazzle their eyeballs that had been waiting to discover, here at the backyard of the Nirvana, a more spectacular truth.

With the peculiar gold brocade around the edges and lily flowered stones embedded on all fronts, it looked similar to a queen's make-up trunk that was buried along as her last wish.

"How can such a thing on Earth have something that is mystic?" Audin could sense the feminism that lingered around the box. The art of philosophy and the masculine ways of power were never to be associated to women by him, and so the box had to have something that was adorable or signifying beauty. Had he already committed the first mistake?

"On a count of three?" Audin was ready to flap it open.

"No...let's take it to your room, not here." Rama gave the suggestion seriously.

"As you say, fill in the soil and come upstairs." Rama's soul deserted him as he saw Audin quickly leaving the crime scene.

"But?" But there was no answer. Rama was to mop the spilled vomit of indigestible curiosity and fear.

He looked back at the open gate with the awe of a half-alive victim chased by a serial killer.

"How could he?" Rama made himself available with the two naked choices- he was either to run away and suspend for the moment thinking about the mysterious box or to pick the shovel, step inside, and re-pack the grave. But it was not as simple as it sounded, for there were many other things besides lifting the pile of sand –there was the cat, and her kittens, and there were names of dead men written on the headstones which he may read however much he tried not to; there were spider webs loaded with insects that were still throbbing; there was a crevice in the wall that looked like the sky of the judgement day with an eye-like opening. The list was long and undefeatable. Rama fled away, breathing less thinking more about all the excuses that he may produce at the event of being questioned about the unclosed door and the unfilled trench. He was waiting for Audin's call. The devotional rhyme played once again but not matching his musical run.

"No, no, I had to go. She was yelling!" Rama tried to hide the incompetence of his lungs, he had been eating air.

"I'll come tomorrow, and if not, let's meet on Sunday."

"Yes, I can wait. I probably know what's going to be in there." Audin said at ease, he was a gentleman always at ease. In fact, the discovery of box, in the backyard room, had not surprised him at all; he was perhaps taking his time to understand this unfamiliar way of experimenting on 'things' that never spoke, unlike humans- his age old specimens.

Audin placed the box on the table decoratively and laid himself on the bed. The conditioned air had been fine, perfectly fine for his fatigued body; sleep was a distant dream though not to be realized this soon. He gazed at the ceiling, then at the table, and then again gazed at the ceiling, as if both of them, he and the box, were playing spelling bee in a strange sign language.

I should stop thinking about the box, and talking to myself. I must sleep.

Irrespective of whether or not man is evolving, it is certain that he has the ability to evolve one piece of occurrence into another- it's about insomnia. A happening of past, the past being few hours old, still warm, evolves into a gluey larvae that can crawl up a nape, which evolves into a jumbled fabric of cocoon that can mar a scalp, which evolves into a moth that can buzz around eyes, all of these don't die away they only disappear when you have given up on the struggle to sleep. How skilful of us! Or '*silk-full*' rather! Audin changed his sleeping position from the latitudes to the longitudes, from one diagonal of the bed to another, tried a couple of different pillows after being satisfied with the compromised position, and finally found out that he was feeling cold.

Where is my shirt? Ah, I left it there on the grave. Wait, why am I thinking about the backyard? I have so many to wear.

The insomniac closed his eyes, let the lines of distress on his forehead even out, and said, "A wooden box, one box should not knock me down so easily." By now, he had realized that the big question was not about proving others, or Rama, false; it was about the survival of his own conviction, and 'universal' ideas. Any loophole would not be spared- it would be cut down to pieces and served with meal three times a day. He must not forget this.

And then an oral questionnaire was prepared in the conditioned air, by him, to be answered by himself, and if he answered all of them in his favour he may not have to suffer more sleepless nights.

Let me back-track the events if the box is proven to be supernatural in the days to come. The last day says that the box does not belong to this 'material' universe. The day before the last day lays down substantial proofs for that to happen. So, backtracking, the first day should have one piece of evidence in favour of the last day, however much small. Has something peculiar happened today, before-while-after discovering the box? The cat? No. What else? Almost nothing, as logical as every other day, as sequential as a rat trap mechanism.

Since whatever has happened was fairly predictable, I must deal with the existence of the components of every argument that has been brought under my sight. I dissect the primary definitions. The first subject, here, must be the mystic powers! How am I supposed to dissect this? Can we add or subtract powers from a theoretical point of view? Or are these unchanging? If there exists a power, a mystic power, there must exist someone who possessed that power, or else the display of 'power' without personification would be no more than a natural phenomenon! Like glittering of gold! Like free flowing of water! An extraordinary physical phenomenon when personified, or associated with a mortal person, might be thought of as mystic power. I think, yes. A piece of wood would float in water- a natural phenomenon; a person who can float on water against his natural phenomenon but following the wood's natural phenomenon would be believed to possess mystic powers.

But then, since natural phenomena can be easily combined or separated, powers must also be able to get combined or separated. If that is true, then there must be someone who can entertain multiple natural phenomena simultaneously i.e. has multiple powers, and then there should be someone with multiple powers with a larger degree, and then someone who has all kinds of power, with the largest degree, and then the one with the infinite kinds of powers with the infinite degree! Master of following all the natural phenomena- his and the rest! Would he be Rama's God? The he or the she? The God or the Goddess?

Rama's God manufactured the Earth; he manufactured other friends of Rama, other humans in his own image. Most senseless! And least creative! Then created all other beings with similar behaviours, and dropped all of us on the Earth as tenants with a short-service agreement; whoever doesn't abide by the rules must be reprimanded, and whoever does must be rewarded. A very inefficient strategy, I must say. Well, this is not expected from someone who possesses the infinite forms of powers. That is not acceptable at all. It is almost a fraud, prima facie.

I should shut myself up. It is a one foot wide wooden box which may break into pieces if sneezed on, and, which got so useless that it had to be buried, and now I am being influenced to adopt this orphan- a by-product of sensationalism, to exile my own child! A box with a guide to controlling natural phenomena! I am going to do this for my father, a duty, a last wish and no more than that, since he had so much confidence in me. Perhaps, I have interpreted his words wrongly, very wrongly; could it be that his ulterior motive was only to prove to everyone the real superstitious nature of this box! I think I am going too far and too fast. Let me open it first! What if it contains dead rats?

He flung out of the bed like a morning alarm and switched on all of the lights; it was 2 a.m., then pulled out the old mahogany chair and sat in line with the box that rested breathlessly on the table as if a patient waiting for the surgeon to operate upon him.

Audin slid open the window to have a look at the Ridge trees, this always inspired him.

Every human starts framing his own mental pictures about the world soon after the day he is born. The journey of his life moves on the tracks laid by these pictures, which get diverged in two more tracks-the good and the bad or the "to be followed" and the "not to be followed." The entities falling in one category may slip into the other category; the pictures keep on changing as he looks from side to side asking directions. The marijuana that once bore the disrespect of a passer-by becomes the source of immense pleasure one day - the bad picture just transformed into the good picture. The lover who was once adored lavishly by her becomes licentious when he finds his consort elsewhere- the good picture just transformed into the bad picture. And thus the two classes of men appear- the first class that is not at all concerned for any of the pictures or its transformation, and spends life in a state of near unconsciousness; and the second- affected by each one, its transformation and spends life differentiating one from the other.

Neither of the classes is able to put an end to the picture story; none is able to find the absolute picture.

Audin, definitely, was an inseparable part of the second class and Rama too for that matter, to some degree. Both of them had an arrangement of pictures about life inspired by everything ever heard, seen, or felt; and both of them believed their collection of pictures to be absolute. This very notion of being absolute, or faultless, gave birth to the fear of being defective or being proven baseless, or being proven picture-less!

It is true; I should think of this as a duty.

Audin's collection of atheistic pictures was a little anxious for being overcast by Rama's collection.

The box had a casual latch that even a sleep-walker could have opened. With no resistance it lay before him revealing what it had been concealing in its stomach for so many years.

That was easy.

A silky blue cloth was chock-a-block in the box in layers, as predicted in the diary. Audin felt his father instructing him throughout. The silk had been of majestic quality and was inscribed with Persian letters. Inside the layers, there was present, a thicket of plates that appeared to have been made of gold and in the shape of Peepal tree leaves.

They are so many of them, and nearly weightless.

The thicket was sewn along the stalk without any thread or any visible adhesive making it look like a small brochure. Every leaf manufactured with tolerance in microns, maybe smaller, and with extruded surfaces.

I am holding this in my hand, which the great King himself handed over to Sir James Stewart. I don't think this is so hallucinating that it should put someone in solitary confinement. And let me assure myself about it being not so astonishing as not to be called a historical artwork. Amazing artistry indeed!

He wanted to call Rama, but didn't. "Rama wouldn't have slept, must be expecting to meet one of the dead Englishmen in his toiled compound." He said staring at the still forests.

Chapter 6

Audin Stewart flipped the next metallic plate over the golden thread. It was the last one, and there were a total of twenty seven, marvellous twenty seven!

All Greek to me, like this soft chirping of birds!

A family of woodpeckers, resting on the branches, was least amused by this bumptious presence under their tree.

It had been 4:30 am, and the light was the dimmest in the Ridge. *Reading in low light can give you a headache,* he had heard at school; nothing was said, though, about reading an incomprehensible script.

Leaving the book of plates on the boulder he had been sitting on for an hour, he stood a meter away to observe it, agilely removing his spectacles - a movement that was synonymous to the darting eyes of a child when he starts looking at one corner of the ceiling to trace unwritten answers. He was not being himself. Although the scattered leaves, the boulder, and the sky were self-absorbed and completely unaware of him, Audin doubted each one of them of causing some secret disturbance.

I could not sleep last night; maybe that is the reason.

This was the least frequented part of the forest, guarded against the banging feet of joggers and chit-chat of the retirees; overgrown with vegetation, shady, peaceful, and free of synthetics that spoke of humans. There were only two communities of people that risked coming this deep – the drug addicts who wanted to throw themselves on the ground like a free fall to remain unconscious and unidentified for days, and emotional adolescent couples who were desirous of knowing their counterparts physically; for the rituals of both had been socially objectionable if performed overtly. At this hour, Audin was the sole occupant and there was no sign of the coming of the patrons of any of the communities.

A line of black ants emerging out of the roots of the tree followed his attention. Uplifting any edible that hit their path, it marched disciplinarily towards his slippers and disappeared in a pre-decided tunnel; perhaps it had been a morning practice. The world that lived on the ground had been unassumingly organised, much more elaborate and complex than the one watching it carelessly. An idler may spend an entire day noting the inhabitants, before finally lifting his gaze up for bird-watching. Quite similar complexities were displayed by the metallic book. The left plate had extruded round surfaces, without any pattern, but of variety of sizes as minuscule boulders, and on the right had been Sanskrit texts, written so finely that they could barely be read or as if not meant to be read at all. Audin ventured to analyse it all over again - this needed the indomitable will of a bee that knows everything but still steeps her nest in honey only to be consumed by someone else.

The perfection in shape of the texts is reminiscent of descriptive works of Italian artists, and the haphazard hemispheres make it look like the big-bang ejaculating universes. Every inference is contradictory with others. Uh, let's think afresh. The left, the right. The written, the drawn. The texts might be the Sanskrit hymns of Hindus that Rama often talks about, parallel to which is a left page that is perhaps the pictorial representation of the hymn. Each left has a right that explains the left or vice versa. That makes a total of thirteen pairs, and, one spare plate!

There was, undoubtedly, a single plate, the last one that had no corresponding page of hemispheres.

Where's the last one - lost over a period of time, keeping in mind the number of hands that were laid here? What could be the most obvious story behind this - A goldsmith worked himself into a lather to mould a raw piece of gold to this shape for Aurangzeb who made it a present to one of his proud wives, and then upon rejection, it fell into Sir

James Stewart's palms along with the mysticism tale? This lacks sensation; obvious stories need to have that sensational element to take them forward. Why would the king have needed to fabricate a tale?

I remember reading it once that the emperor Aurangzeb once inscribed a Quran with his hands, with his own tool-set. So, it might be safe, a thin wafer of safety, to conclude that he himself did this thing. No, the wafer's too crispy to sustain- he was a staunch follower of Islam, and must have been loath to even think of Hinduism, could never have inscribed Sanskrit on something; Persian or maybe Arabic was acceptable. So, if it was so, why would any Hindu saint offer him something that was a "good" mascot for him? The wafer has been munched.

I am heading nowhere. I am rafting in a river. I must either find the spring- the beginning, or the ocean- the end, to be able to nurture the feeling of having reached somewhere.

His memory had been razor-sharp. Anything ever heard, said, or read never escaped the clutches of his mind, which he later used to modulate his or other's arguments. This capability had indeed hardened the foundations of his atheistic philosophies.

This introspection captured his senses so well that he never realized that a drug addict, the first category patrons, had bumped himself on the opposite boulder, very near, and that he had already begun his rituals.

He was a puckered face writ large by his grey beard that had grown in all dimensions, clothed with sand

and dirt like an overused mattress which had never been through a dusting. The smeared shirt that he wore was perhaps shoplifted from a coal mine, with pockets on the chest, and a torn half sleeve on the left arm that juxtaposed with the full sleeve on the right; distinct proof of a severe beating that he might have received lately. He took out a needle from his knickers, very slackly, as if his fractured hands were still aching, tearing the plastic covering that was meant to be thrown but not on Audin.

His rough, long hair was falling on his eyes blocking his vision like a fish-net. The transparent cover landed on the golden plates. Audin picked the cover and saw out of it a wretched man sitting in front, with a wounded leg, playing with a needle. He was as amazed to see him as the woodpeckers had been some hours ago. The drug addict was appreciably patient in performing his rituals like the ants that had passed by Audin's feet.

"Good morning." Audin tried to introduce himself forwarding his hand, "I am Audin; I live in the street across."

The drug addict was never welcomed with such warmth, "Hmmm?" His eyes were bulging out, as if he had never been cured of a life-long tuberculosis and was about to die.

"Are you alright? Will you drink some water? It's fresh."

"Hmmm, no, is it morning? Good morning..."he looked up to ensure the presence of dispersed light.

The festering wound on his knee was the feast to a cloud of flies that was hovering passionately as if there could not have been a better breakfast - dead skin, pus, and blood were being served. He toppled his boulder, under which he had hidden his belongings yesterday.

"Do you visit this place often?" Audin noticed the buried syringe.

"uh...yes," he stumbled, "...and you?"

"I jog here, on the outer tracks, regularly. I have come to this side for the first time."

"American? That big white house is yours? " The drug addict fixed the needle into the syringe.

"No, I am an Indian; I have been here for nearly twenty years. You are quite a frequent wanderer?"

"Very rich. Why do you come here? It's dangerous for you..." He unsealed a packet that seemed to have white tablets to mix with a brown solution.

"If you could see this...this is a kind of a book that I found buried in my backyard. My father said it had mystic powers, and he wanted me to do something about it. What do you think? Possibly true? " Audin thought he had no reason to conceal anything from him, or from anyone; despite his father's warning, he revealed every minute detail, just like he did to Bhola Prasad.

"You don't have to earn your living; that's why you bother about this."

"Even you don't have to. What would you do if you were in my place?"

"This?" The drug addict asked if he may have a look at the thing.

"...and how did you get this wound?" Audin handed over the book, heavily concentrating on amoebic flesh.

"It looks gold, uh? Would you like to sell it, Am-ree-kan?"

"No, I am afraid I cannot, how did you get this wound?" Audin repeated.

"Ha! I don't return this, what can a sissy like you do at all?"

"Nothing!"Audin repeated the question as if he was sure to receive a breath-taking revelation.

"Tell me what could the Am-ree-kan do if I run away now!"

"Before you do that you must tell me about this wound?"

"I was beaten by a bastard on the crossroad. Badly..., with a hockey stick."

"And you talk of running away!" Audin said looking deep into his eyes. The drug addict laughed heartily, forgetting that his damaged teeth were now visible, a souvenir awarded by the hockey player. No one had in fact talked to him, verbally, with this much interest in many years.

"People stay away from me. That must happen to you as well, uh?"

"There is nothing strange in that, it doesn't happen to me though. So, how do you take it? You are good about it?"

"I keep myself intoxicated. I don't know who I am talking to; I don't know what I do; I don't know what I speak; I don't know what I see; I don't fear anyone, no one! Not even the Am-ree-kan! Isn't that enough?"

"You talk sensibly, so you must be thinking sensibly. You are good. But where do you get money from? For this equipment, and these medicines?"

"Am I talking sensibly? Uh! I haven't had dosages yet. Nothing. And I sold one kidney; got more than two lakhs; it's a hefty amount. See!" The drug addict had been carrying a thick wad of five hundred rupee notes; he, indeed, didn't fear anyone.

"Why do you take drugs then?"

"That's a bad question. I tell you, a bad question ruined your personality. Why would a drug addict be called a drug addict if he takes no drugs? Ha! Though I would not mind being called something else!" He waived the packet, "It is a choice."

"Why do, then, people beat you, like this?"

"They say it's unacceptable. Intoxication is wrong; everywhere. People are telling their children that this is wrong. Tell me, would you like your wife to bear child that comes out of her puffing on a cigarette! Ha!"

"No, I would not. But intoxication is another form of pleasure, so that makes it a kind of necessity. So, as you rightly said, it is about choice. Some choose to be intoxicated, or pleasured, by the money, some by the power or the fame, some by the beauty. And others who have lost faith in all of the three things I just mentioned, pleasure themselves with drugs or these liquids. This is transient; the first one lasts for years. Now, you tell me, would you find it justifiable if a drug-intoxicated man is being chased by a power-intoxicated? They both are on the same ground, with same desires, same hormones."

"You are... I think I would make a good playmate for your intoxicated children, if you have any." The man had suspended his rituals.

"No, I have no children, but I am against intoxication of any kind and every kind, because it destroys you physically, with bleak chances of recovery, so it doesn't really serve the pleasure-purpose that well. Basically, it's a bad bargain."

"I lost my wealth, my family, and everything, and I took refuge in these. Eight years ago. I lost them. And the rest of it, what was left...anyways. It was destiny, there is not much you can do about it, destiny is like a butt, cigarette butt- you hate it but it holds everything that you want to hold on to."

"Destiny," Audin had ridiculed this word many times before; he verified again, "Destiny?"

"Yes. One who was once a powerful businessman is now a beggar. I would have bought this entire turf of land."

"That was quite disappointing. I believed you decided what you wanted to be and have become that. You give credit of this hard earned position to a fictitious destiny. My father wrote in his valedictory letter that I start wondering about destiny. How can we? Isn't that a mental weakness?"

"The lines that have been written are written excruciatingly hard. God is the balancer- bad in bad, good in good; you can't get away from him. Would you mind reading my palm-lines?" The palm had been as dark as the dorsal, and there were hardly any lines; it would be adulatory to say that such a hand could have been able to pump a syringe in any way.

"No, I am sorry, I cannot. Why does he fit so well in the seat of a balancer, as per you? How did he get elected? I have seen people balancing on ropes, rope-walkers! They depend on people around them, their subjects. In fact, every balancer depends upon his subjects, so that dependency makes God very vulnerable. That's a bad answer. You are ruined, I tell you, a bad answer ruined your personality!" But the drug addict was busy twisting his palms as a rubber band to see any visible line, and rubbing them against each other.

"You ask questions! You don't talk. You ask questions! I must leave from here. You are being a headache! You will not let me enjoy the moments of pleasure!" He pushed his legs against the ground, strained the wound, and managed to stand himself up. "...and don't follow me!"

"I am sorry if I am being a headache. You can take your dosages. I won't stop. You have been...nice to me."

"But you have been a headache! Am-ree-kan!" He didn't look back, and kept repeating. His left sleeve was synchronously walking with the right one, and that appeared to Audin to be the motion of the left and right plates of the book.

"Wait. I think you have my book." Audin left his boulder.

"I told you not to follow me, not to follow me! Stay away from me or I will punch you in the face. And a lost man's punch is real bad." The glitter of the edge of the book, lying in the burrow beneath the opposite boulder struck Audin's eye and he felt he had offended the man but he continued to follow, and soon emulated his languorous pace. "I apologize."

"Look. I am going to have this. I can answer your questions, but you will have to have it too...along with me, here, now...now! Ha!" The drug addict was willing to share his expensive diet with the new friend who had encroached upon his haven. That is an astounding trait of the intoxicating fraternity- helping one other to dilute the pains of life.

Audin, without a faint sign of distrust, accepted the proposal. "I will, but I have not done this before." The needle was no sharper and longer than those that entertained blood samples. "I am sure you are expert at it."

"Keep calm, and fix your eyes. Look how I do this!"

He mixed a powdery content to a liquid that was colourless, and from his hairy ear canal he plugged out a small cotton swab that was greasy in texture and mustard in colour. With the exactness of a robotic arm, he sucked in the solution out of the cotton, and the dish was ready to serve.

"Boy! You or me?"

"As you say." Audin gave out his hand.

"The guest!" The needle subtly penetrated his white skin to release the nectar; the nectar that was going to put him in the state of highest pleasure. The drug addict then injected himself.

"How much time does it take?" Audin was curious to know how much time he had to put his final questions before they both fall down. He was indifferently waiting to savour the hallucinating dish, for his piece of cake was the vibrant words of this drug addict.

"It lasts for three hours on me..."

"No, when does it actually start to make some effect."

"Five seconds..." he replied to remain unheard. The unconscious body of the millionaire, Audin Stewart, had collapsed down at the feet of the wretch. The time that lapsed afterwards was immeasurable, slower than a stopped clock, and more comforting than a utopian vacation.

The drug addict was liberated, for the time being, of this day's fight to find a reason to live, of the pains of society, and of the agonising memories; everything had juiced down to cipher. And Audin had himself become a part of the specimen that he was experimenting on, discretionally diving in the same river for which he had forbidden, in fear of drowning, the river's fish.

The place, in any way, had not been worth treading on as it was teeming with earthworms and their excreta, and a few grams of pigeon droppings everywhere; however, both of them had propped themselves against the wild shrubs, and dreamt of sprawling on a bed of roses. The metallic book lied a metre away, unattended, like a ripe fruit just fallen off the tree.

The lunch hour at the factory had gotten over; Rama couldn't find his companion whom he was phoning from the time the machines were switched on for the day. Each time, the call got picked up by Bhola Prasad who denied knowing a living person with such a name and said, "I had known someone called 'Audin;' he used to come here, but he died last week."

Bhola Prasad happened to pass by the same part of the Ridge, to shoo off the first and second category patrons, if any, and to cut away the overgrown vegetation. He saw the two heads hanging effortlessly along the broad shrubs, and shouted, "You have come again? You have come again? You drunkard! I will kill you! I told you to find some other place, and that doesn't mean the other place of this forest! People are going to complain against me, don't you understand? I will lose my job! ", "Wait! You wait there! It is your last day on the earth!"

Bhola Prasad snapped off a branch, and swung it like a mace to lash the drug addict's bare feet.

"Wake up! I will injure your right leg too! And who is this? You are enjoying with your friends here? Is this a tavern? You morons!" He kicked at Audin's back, and upturned his face with his weapon.

"O God! I should have known it! I should have known it; this Englishman has to have some connection with this drunkard! Wake up! Or I am calling the police!" An "ahead of time" warning was issued.

Multiple images of trees, a man, and another man with sticks merged into three distinct images as Audin rolled up his bleary eyes.

"This time you are caught!"

Audin observed his surroundings; his collar drenched in saliva, Bhola Prasad was shouting at him, a bearded man was staring half-awake, and the hands of the clock suggested it was evening. His consciousness continuously unfolded the series of events that he had experienced.

"Uh, what? How, have you...been?" Audin had woken up after a sound sleep of more than half a day. He looked for the metallic book that had been the sole reason of this adventurous ride.

"I am calling the police! And don't think you can get away because you are rich!" Bhola Prasad goaded Audin's face with his stick.

"Police? Somebody stole my phone."

"I do not have your phone!" Bhola Prasad shouted repeatedly, and scurried away with a weird jugglery of feet.

"Uh...I am sorry...I have forgotten your name... "Audin attempted to continue the suspended discussion upfront.

"Call me anything. Why are you still here? I see you haven't left... I know you want another drive." The drug addict could not think of anything else, and was readying himself for the dinner.

"No, thank you. You promised me to answer my questions. Before this..."

"Go ahead."

"You said your God is a 'balancer.' Could you elaborate on that?"

"I don't know I said that. I did not say he is the balancer. Did I ever say that? You can leave now; I have to urinate." He was irritated for being woken up midway.

"Yes, I will, soon. But how will you justify that such a God who is influenced by his subjects, very undoubtedly, can take a decision that is not flawed? Isn't the God too much obsessed by this autocratic freak?" The drug addict began to urinate in a manner that suggested that he had no control over it.

"So, how will you justify yourself?" Audin was talking to his back.

"You see this? See, see this? Is it worried about its path? It is just spreading, crawling, and filling up those burrows! Are you listening to this poem? Don't wait boy! I am not gonna answer! You can leave now, or I would slam those shining window panes of your house! Stones all over!" The drug addict had a sharp conviction in his last statement that made Audin wind up dissatisfied. He paid him the amount worth the dosage and headed for his home, "It was pleasure meeting you, Mister?"

"Mister? Mistress." the wretch replied kicking the wet ground.

Chapter 7

The metallic plates had bedazzled the minds sufficiently, becoming the source and the sink of philosophical discussions at the same time. On a general agreement, when the arguments of both had acquired dry and cliché overtones, the malady was timely referred to a practitioner who could make a conclusion in favour of either party; the two men otherwise would have shamelessly titled the sterile mule a male horse or a female donkey.

Dr Junaed Sayiid headed the Applied Physics department at the University, and had worked with the Indian Space Research Organisation for nine years. Rama, once his ingenious student and surrendered follower during the graduate days, presented to him the thicket of plates, expecting a personal favour that demanded a thorough research on its elemental structure. Dr Sayiid conducted more than twenty experiments, sparing precious time from his monotonous profession, to dovetail his findings.

Instead of handing over the bundle of reports, he asked Rama to meet him in person and soon.

In a cane chair, the scientist sat quietly with the emotionless-ness of a sloth, waiting for sleep to intervene to make his torso fall flat on the table. Rama appeared in front of the half opened door.

"Hmm...Rama? I was not expecting you today..." He nodded his big head, which was so perhaps to accommodate his big nose and big eyes, giving them the privilege to sit. After pushing his heavy hands against the weak arms of the chair, he walked up to the cupboard, affording a limp. Being a serious diabetic, his left foot was swollen and could not be used or even touched; the faded jeans that he wore were always rolled up to his knees to expose the diseased part.

"I came in as soon as I could. Audin is my friend. The plates are his."

"Good evening, sir."

"Hmm..."He nodded again, as if conserving his energy by minimizing the use of his tongue.

"The piece had been very surprising." He opened up the thick file of freshly printed papers, and the plates.

"Piece?"

"The plates," Rama silenced Audin, and then said to Mr Sayiid, "He is a graduate in literature."

"Literature?" The voice in which he spoke showed his disliking for such lowly subjects and that he would never make an eye contact with such a man again.

"Rama, and you, the piece, here, is a masterpiece." He was bulging out his eyes for no reason.

"It has a nice mixture of properties of metals and a few non-metals. If I tell you in layman's terms, since you're a student of literature, the plates shine like gold but are not gold. They are very hard and very light but are not plastic. It is exceptionally surprising, if you understand what I just mentioned."

"I understand that, sir."

Dr Sayiid jumped to the page that displayed a massively zoomed picture of the piece. "Can you see the surface? The text written on it is extruded. And the extrusions have been found hollow. The hemispheres are hollow, too. That is again exceptionally surprising."

"Hollow? That's too small to be hollow."

"That's not small, we call it microscopic. It cannot be a mere coincidence that the radius of every hemisphere, in millimetres, is numerically equal to 2.725."

"2.275?"

"The distance between the hemispheres is in the multiple of 2.275, and the thickness of each is approximately 0.2275, impossible to produce artificially by any techniques known. The point here is that the ratio of the radii of the Moon to the Earth is 0.2725. I call it mathematical symmetry. And that is again exceptionally surprising."

"So what do you conclude, sir?" Audin was not able to form any mental picture with the information just fed in, and was thinking of an answer that was decisive, after all it was why he had agreed to Rama for this post-mortem.

"Conclusion, here, is not the summary of a passage, son. That is why I teach, and love physics, and not literature! Let me continue, if you are kind enough to let me?

"And please do not flaunt that smile; the matter here is of dire seriousness." Nothing in his life was worth giving a smile or laugh; it was, rather, a conduct of vagabonds.

"The extruded surface, that is the hemispheres, has been detected hollow, as they have two reflecting surfaces. This could have been done either by extruding the bubbles from the other side of the plate or by directly welding them onto the plates. The latter suggestion is more probable, but a welding technique this fine is yet to be discovered because there are no visible burrs or signs of metallic fusion even at microscopic level."

"I will show you a thing. Could you read the text, Rama?" He upturned the golden plates over the seam carefully as if they formed a live pigeon.

"Yes. But I may not be able to translate it."

"And the person sitting adjacent to you, can he read?"

"...ah...no, sir. I noticed this on the day I found it."

"And of course you would not be aware of why it is so. A paper reflects light, diffusively, in all directions thus can be read at any angle. Here, at the surface of plates, the reflection is so very much fine-tuned that the person reading it must make a right angle to its plane. At any other angle you would never see the extruded text. I may suggest, and not "conclude", that this was to make the reader extremely meticulous; which means some high-importance information was being shared."

"What else can you suggest?"

"What do you suggest, Audin; is that your name?"

"Yes. I think it is an intricate artwork, and..."

"No," Dr Junaed interjected, emphasizing, "This masterpiece was developed by a highly advanced civilization; that, I don't know how or why, had techniques far superior to present day; thus, this is not an artwork of a popular goldsmith; that is nearly an accusation. You don't have to transform science into art to accept its excellence."

"I accept its excellence, sir. I appreciate science."

"I would also like to comment that there has to be an encrypted meaning to the hemispheres. Pondering over the mathematical symmetry, this may represent some other planetary system or even a universe. And many other assumptions can be made, but before declaring anything, I will send it to the National Material Science Laboratory for further experimentation. Then, probably, to the Archaeological Survey of India to decrypt the signs of a Sanskrit speaking civilization that wrote on Peepal leaves. It will be interesting to know, at least for me, what transpires."

It is not a far-fetched idea! It might land in a museum.

"That's not the requirement, I think. Your research has been of great help, sir, but I must leave now. Thanks, thank you...for... it, your time." Audin scurried out of the room, depositing the plates back in his pockets.

"That was sheer disrespect!" Dr Sayiid's face squirmed, like a plum crushing itself in anger.

"I apologize, that is highly...disrespectful. I will bring him up..."

Audin had swept out of the building in minutes; for he felt a multitude of scientists chasing him to seize what lied in his pockets.

"Will you slow down?"

"Will you!"

"This old man...this old man invested...so much time and effort on this; at least pose a sincere, thankful mouth to him!"

Rama went out of breath, and perched himself on a parked motorcycle. Audin double backed.

"He wants to distribute the 'piece' among his fraternity. I regard what he said, and that this is beyond an artwork."

"You could have gracefully come out of the room. People don't even get to meet him."

"What if I meet him again, now, to apologize?"

"Did you see that empty vase on his table?"

"Yes."

"He would smash that on your head."

"I regret what happened, but he would have made this thing a part of national property. My father warned about it; I should have realised." They stood up to walk towards the exit gate.

"What is the problem, then, in realising when your father said *'this book is a source of mysticism'*? And close this case right here. As easy as that! No more circus!"

"He himself did not want me to realize that, that's simple to understand."

"You have become an over-thinker. Whatever Dr Sayiid has revealed makes the question of this book being a mundane item of a pawnshop, out of context. Science cannot explain everything, and it certainly cannot remove your mental blocks. There is a limit. Rishi ji once told that mysticism can explain science, to the deepest level, but science cannot even enter the realm of mysticism."

"It often strikes me that your life, your thoughts, your ideologies, and even your mental blocks are all influenced by Rishi ji. If I ever get to meet him I won't find a new individual but a...a precocious self of yours."

"I have accepted him as my spiritual master."

"Does it help?"

"There is no other way. When the subject matter is new, whatever part of it you claim to have understood is either influenced from a book or a master; even the book is an indirect reference to the master. What is abnormal about it?"

"There is nothing abnormal but over a period of time you may lose your sense of speculation."

"Speculation? You speculated on this book for two weeks, and could not near a substantial inference."

"So, I think, in the next two minutes you would suggest that I surrender unto Rishi ji, and he would help me find the truth."

"One hundred percent, he is the knower of Vedas; he is a mystic himself."

"What if it is just a 'value judgement'?"

"No, it won't be, or I would unlearn everything, and renounce this world!"

Chapter 8

Chindauli is a sleeping village in western Haryana. And had been much so twelve years ago when Rama wedded to Jhelum. She was infamously titled as the harridan-queen of the village then - a woman does not need to push her limits to fight inequality, being natural and a little humorous would suffice - Jhelum was neither, but then, she had killed men. Many incidents of her life, when she was a maiden, became an inseparable part of the anecdotal history of the village. Driving a farm tractor across the sloping streets was one of her favourite pastimes, and this she learned out of the desperate need to drive Raavi to her husband's home. There was no male member in the family but Mehtab, her father. Her grandfather had stopped considering himself a part of this family though he still comfortably lived with them.

In the expectancy of a boy, the family of hers got extended to nine members; all the five girls were named after the rivers of Punjab - Chenab, Raavi, Beas, Sutlej, and Jhelum. Each of them, eventually, got married in consecutive years but finding a bridegroom for her took inordinately long. Though

Mehtab had been a policeman, and maintaining a family of nine had not been that troublesome, but the maidenhood of his eldest daughter became a subject of grapevine criticism; a problem for which the society itself was responsible more than the "stout" girl.

"Mehtab's home? We are from Jilwana village." The prospective bridegroom's father stopped a young cyclist laden with milk drums who had been in an unstoppable flurry of locomotion.

"Jilwana village? There is no relative of his in that village; I know him for years; you must be mistaken."

"I am mistaken! I am the head of the bridegroom's family. I want to meet him as early as possible, which way should I go?" It was considered a bad practice to upset any character of the bridegroom's family, and this man had been overly familiar with the rule.

"Bridegroom? Are you marrying your son to her... his eldest daughter?"

"Why are you so concerned? You are a milkman, behave like one."

"Uh! Recede! If you are to take my advice, and if you and your son are to live peacefully. Haven't you heard she has gotten refused five times? She is the eldest; why do you think Mehtab could not manage to marry her to someone?" The cyclist alighted from the vehicle and sat down on the street-side platform to have the privilege of revealing Jhelum's chronicles inside out.

"He did not tell us any such thing. We were told she teaches in a primary school, and is the youngest. We have been kept in the dark! Does he imagine that I am a wayfarer surviving on his doles?"

"Sit down here; I will let you know everything. His home is still afar..."

"That girl, Jhelum; she doesn't even have a brother..." The cyclist had been an opportunist story teller, and selling milk evolved into an uninteresting side-business.

"...and there is much more to tell. Even that child, there! Even he can recite to you all of her deeds. I don't know what lured you into his schemes."

"He promised me a motorcycle."

As years went by, or as she grew tons of muscles on her arms, many tales got appended to the Jhelum's chronicles, each superseding the amazement of the last edition. Had a seasoned documentary film-maker shot her in action, he would have debunked every scene for being 'scripted'.

Usually, the tales had been a medium of bringing embarrassment to the family, but once, in the winter of 1998, Jhelum's bravery fairly watered down the defamation of Mehtab's, without being aimed to do so, and her name got inked on the front page of the local newspaper.

Jhelum was in a habit of smoking hookah – her grandfather's scared possession in these decaying years; it was the one and the only occupation where he was able to engage his senses and mind simultaneously. Before putting himself to bed, every night, the old man would load the hookah bowl with tobacco and new coals to ready it for the coming day's sessions. But he was often heard shouting, "Where has the tobacco gone? Did it burn itself! Who touched it! Have you all gone deaf?" If only walls could answer to the coughing chest! The old man was compelled to blame his age that he thought had made him senile and he would soon die of brain failure.

She would wake up before the larks to lock herself in the walled buffalo-shed where her grandfather hid the hookah. Undoubtedly, this was the most appropriate time for this fine act of pilfering smoke; the air was so sleep inducing, and the light with only such a miserly presence that a kindergarten child trying to tell a buffalo from a man would always fail.

She had had the time of her life when others were snoring in their rooms- as if they were beans, left in a rectangular bowl to be soaked overnight; even the buffalos had put their mechanical rumination to rest.

It had almost been a month; now she was equally handy to her grandfather. In her naïve days it used to take her an hour to set ablaze the coals, produce the vital smoke out of the tobacco. The shed had got a temporary construction, with too many gaps between the bricks that faced the street, perhaps to channel the air in and out. She was intelligent enough to choose this part of the house as her playground; every trace of the fresh smoke got ventilated out before being detected by snorting noses, and the bubbling sound of the hookah could be easily mistaken for the bellowing of one of the dumb buffalos in case someone was awake.

The fitful gushes of wind on that morning of December were putting off the flaming coals, and, despite wearing a woollen shawl, the freezing weather gave her the feeling to enclose herself under the warm hookah bowl. She pulled on the first whiff, a gallon of smoke was inhaled, and she could feel the settling warmth in her throat and chest. The bubbling of water was kept sufficiently low. She pulled on another one, and was enjoying more than she could have while lying asleep purposelessly.

A thud!

She heard a thud, not common at this time.

Oh! Not now! Where is the manger?

The manger was filled to the brim with fodder; Jhelum stashed away the live hookah urgently into it, too careless to notice that flaring coals may burn the dry fodder. The water tank, in one corner, from where the cattle drank was open. Jhelum unhesitatingly gargled her throat to stifle the tobacco odour with the viscous water, and then tip-toed near the sash that only had a sack-cloth curtain in the name of a door. She took an easy peep out of the porous sack-cloth. Someone draped in a white bed-sheet, heavily built like an ox and dexterous like a squirrel, was peeping into another room, just like Jhelum; perhaps this world works on this principle of foolish duality- every fool is always being overlooked by another fool, every fool with immense faith in his intelligence believes himself to be in isolation from other fools.

Very shortly, another man, with a custodial temperament that only fatherly brothers display, landed with an identical thud. Jhelum's father had had no such youthful bones to support this kind of jump, and her mother was too sane for such random feats.

Who are these ruffians? I will make this really bad for them!

The elder one had a pistol in his hand.

Jhelum looked about the entire buffalo-shed; there was nothing that could have been improvised as a weapon except the hookah and a wheat bag. The idea of the hookah had to be given up, it wasn't affordable, and the wheat bag was apparently too light to be used for the purpose of asphyxiation.

As expected, she laid herself prostrate on a sleeping buffalo and tried hefting it up, but couldn't really encircle the large trunk.

You coward! Useless animal!

She stamped on her rubbery tail to give her a quick, last-minute scolding.

The dacoits had, by now, decided the room should be barged in, and had lined themselves with their backs touching each other. Jhelum's infuriation was exploding. The crime had already been committed, and it was not the burglary, but the unforgivable suspension of a pleasant hookah play.

As the pistol-man blinked his eyes, Jhelum flung upon him in a murderous spirit, with her left hand choking the veins of his right that held the pistol, and bit his ear off. Her incisors went cutting into his skull, and he screamed many names of God. Pillage with Polytheism!

The choked veins had turned dark blue, and the pistol fell on the ground where the sliced ear lay. In the moment that followed, the younger dacoit kicked her in the buttocks, and then battered her back with his force of two hands.

Realising that her right hand had been unemployed, she poked her fingers into the burglar's eyes. Tears of blood! He whined like a billy-goat whose throat had been left half-cut by a deaf butcher. The other fellow, who, until now, was trying to rescue his brother, felt a stream creeping under his bare foot, and got pushed into a state of ghastliness, as if he had never felt the wetness of blood before – quite unprofessional.

It had been merely fifteen minutes but the screams of Jhelum's victim had awoken the family. Mehtab came out running, with his own gun, and shouted, "Leave him! Jhelum! Jhelum! Leave him! Jhelum!"

"Jhelum!" He, finally, fired a shot in air, which unnecessarily stirred the neighbourhood. The buffalo stood themselves up on their feet unconsciously, like a file of newly recruited soldiers at a commander's whistle. Jhelum felt someone shouting her name, and thus dismounted. She was smeared red. The burglar had already collapsed, lying as soberly as a cemented brick, facing his own pistol, for the first time in his life he could see the back of his ear, though with a single eye.

In the afternoon, the buffalo's skin bore a painful beating by the grandfather's walking stick as he had found his hookah in the manger, and they were the main accused caught red handed. "Do I ever put a covetous eye at your fodder? I would sell all of you! Each one of you! Each and every one of you!"

The incident gained the lady positive popularity; it was then that she came to know about being a policewoman. Amidst this favourable atmosphere in the village, Mehtab met Rama Prasad, whose father had been an ardent follower of Jatharu Rishi, and been seeking a bride for Rama. The innocent Rama, who was in the second year of his graduation at Delhi, had to tie the knot. The ceremony was kept under cover on Rama's relentless request, for he was too 'embarrassed' to reveal that he had married a police woman.

The evening had been darker than it would have been in Delhi; sun sets too early in villages. Here, in Chindauli too, dusk was not a siren of unnatural romance but a susurration of calm and rest as if it was dawn's first cousin.

The Tonga-driver dropped this caravan of three in the middle of the village, for a meagre sum of twenty rupees, owing to Jhelum's one-sided negotiations. A street light was still a distant dream, and not a single bulb was left on before the village lulled itself into sleep. It was about time that the stray dogs performed! And they did so nearly writing half of a sonnet-barking, digging, hopping, howling, licking, panting, roughhousing, and sniffing. They were self-dependent and the world was theirs.

"What is the time? We are late, I suppose." Audin yawned, feeling the stiffness in his body caused by the long journey of Indian railways that can turn your spinal cord upside down.

"Around seven; they must have fallen asleep." Jhelum had stepped in her motherland for the first time after the marriage. She had developed a liking for Delhi as she would enjoy working there with her male colleagues, and get to harass criminals more often.

The ease with which Jhelum was hefting most of the luggage on her broad shoulders made the two men appear like clueless calves being reined away by a cowboy. After covering a distance of more than a hundred meters uphill, they reached an old white house that had two wide entrances, both locked. A large stone platform lay beside each of the entrances; seeing the hand-to-mouth construction of most of the houses its purpose must have been to offer an immediate resting place. And the men seated themselves there. Jhelum palmed the door, threw the luggage on the street, and noticed a long iron rod preventing the door from moving.

"It's locked! I warned you!"

"Should I check the other one? Look, there is some notice...letter..."Audin got off the platform.

A placard was glued on the door, with a flour-paste all around it, that read:

"All the residents of this house have gone on a pilgrimage to the holy shrine of Amarnath; we are the first to do so in the entire village. No one has ever done so in the history of Chindauli, and we are proud of it. We are going to return on the tenth of the next month. Any important message can be written on a paper and be delivered to Ghaal or can be thrown in.

Mehtab"

The placard sounded more like a proclamation and less of information. Rama fancied of this news as a spoof, and that his in-laws would soon open the gate cracking, and he would throw himself on a cot to be dead for the world.

"Didn't you call them before coming?" Audin made an inquisitive face.

"We do not use phones here. Nor do we have television sets or internet connections! You better not curse my village again or I will not allow you to stay here for a moment however much a close friend of Rama you are."

"No, no. I did not mean that. Not at all, I just did not think much before saying that." Audin was still restructuring in his mind his controversial statement that had offended her, and found no loophole in it. While Audin defended himself, she was peeping from the gaps into the buffalo-shed. The manger was empty, and had developed cracks; the pegs that once held the ropes tied around the buffalo were waiting to get uprooted.

He had sold all of them.

"...so, what do we do now? I don't have a problem sitting here, but it is night, it is going to be colder," Audin asked cautiously.

"How could I know? Why are you even asking me?"

"Maybe we can go to Jatharu Rishi's ashram; how far is it from here? If you think...it is right, and we have no other option at hand. We are here to meet him only, I mean... I and Rama...so we can...if you... "Audin gave a sidelong look at Rama who had curled himself into a ball, like a hedgehog.

"We can. Load your luggage; I am not the barber."

"Barber?"

"I am not the barber, either," said Rama, silently, with head propped against the wall and pretending to be in dreams.

"What has it got to do with barbering?" Audin had no idea of what the word was doing here.

"I don't mind shouting at all!" She shook his embryo-ed body vigorously as if he had been her convict sleeping in his working hours.

"Come after me! He lives in the next street, at the end..." The lady had a dominating air, specific to policemen, of always being right and judicious, and thus the men followed as ordered- Audin stooping down under the weight of luggage in the most discomforting gait, and Rama sleep-walking.

The moonlit balconies were casting shadows on the unpaved paths producing beautiful rectangular mazes in the street.

"This side..." Her voice echoed while she was pacing.

And when the men had sufficiently lagged behind so much so that she wasn't visible, Audin hummed an old tune of the Beatles:

"India, India, take me to your heart
Reveal your ancient mysteries to me
I'm searching for an answer, but somewhere deep inside
I know I'll never find it here - it's already in my mind...
I've got to follow my heart wherever it takes me...
I've got to follow my heart wherever it calls to me ..."

"How could you be so undisturbed as to sing a song...?" Rama exhaled in fatigue. Audin continued. The street curved right and reached a dead-end. Jhelum was pointing to an un-plastered house; the boundary walls of which were three- feet high. The absence of doors made it look like it was a public property.

"That one? That's Jatharu Rishi's ashram? A household?" Audin felt let down. His idea of an ashram had been of those he had read in mythological literature- straws, mud floors, and saffron laden disciples with beads on arms, marks on forehead, preparing for the day, where he must reach with great difficulty trespassing dense forests and a river.

There should have been some nuisance, so easy it was. Nuisance is valuable; it is the first testimony of being on a journey.

None of the houses in the village was multi-storeyed or even well-constructed for that matter; all the masons would certainly have complained, if given half a chance, that they were given limited number of bricks that could be used.

Audin Stewart was going to put up here for the next few days or months. Hundreds of miles, literally or figuratively, between the plush mansion of Delhi and an ascetic house in Chindauli.

The walls were painted with a polio advertisement- a poster of black and white children galloping with vivacity. Audin looked all over; most of the area confined by the boundaries had been open- with just two flimsy rooms, a guava tree surrounded by a grassy patch and two cane stools, all betokening simplicity. The place had the lifelessness of a school that caught on fire, children ran away, and teachers got charred.

"What is it?" asked Audin looking all over again in case he missed anything observable.

"It is a school, five classes. I studied here. There I used to play with her..."Jhelum went nostalgic talking about her anonymous friend; seeing her softer side it was hard to accept that she ever had a friend or had survived a school.

"Is Jatharu a teacher?"

"There was no school in the village; he donated his land; he used to sometimes teach yoga to them..." The reverence with which she spoke of the Rishi's philanthropic act was a clear indication of the status he may have enjoyed in the village.

In a corner, an unnoticed man with dark clothes stood alone, staring at the marigold flowers as if he would make a rose out of them. Feeling accompanied, he turned towards the chattering voices; his head was shaven; so were the beard and moustache that gave the impression of a Himalayan monk.

"Swami Ji?" The couple bowed down in respect, and out of a lifelong acquaintance. It appeared that he was the only person, after her parents, whom she undoubtedly regarded. Rama's incomplete genuflection demanded rest for his strained knees.

"Come. Sit. Hmm..." Swami did not sound impatient or surprised at the arrival of visitors at this hour without intimation. Rama sat down on the soil which, finally, provided him with the energy to speak, "Late trains, how ....are you...Swami ji?" He was panting. Audin had been to many parts of India but had never met any sage personally. His mental picture for Jatharu Rishi had been – a dreadlocked hair man under a hundred year old shady tree sitting on a deerskin mat, and meditating beside a river.

It is the philosophy that matters, appearances are nothing but dust.

"Jatharu Rishi is surprisingly young, isn't he?" Audin asked Rama, while Swami searched for chairs in the room.

"He isn't Jatharu Rishi; he must be sleeping."

"Then? I thought he was..." Audin started framing another mental picture, more conservative this time.

"Rishi ji is abed; you can meet him in the morning, I was about to sleep too. I will get you chairs." Swami brought out a cot instead, after all there was not much difference between the two objects as per the laws of austerity. "You must be hungry; there are some fruits." Adjacent to the gate was a hand-pump; Swami fetched a bucketful of water. Jhelum, who was sitting on the cot a moment ago, came out of the other room with lit candles; Audin could now figure out his coordinates in the place, and at what distance he was sitting from the rusty hand-pump, and the entrance, and that the "fruits" being washed were guavas.

"There has been no electricity for ten days. Conditions haven't changed much; electricity is not a regular part of life, but it is fine. God's grace, there are no mosquitoes," Swami offered a pile of ripe guavas "...that room has other cots, quilts; I am going to sleep on the roof; call me if you want something." There was no solid staircase but a wooden ladder that had been missing rungs alternately. Swami climbed up the knackered steps like an injured lizard.

Audin could not understand the relationship between the two.

The God and the mosquitoes! What am I going to ponder over now- may be a duet buzzing. Once upon a time the God graced humans and said, "Let us make man in our image, after our likeness, and let them have dominion over the fish of the sea, and over the fowl of the air, and over the cattle, and over all the earth, and over every creeping thing that creepeth upon the earth.", and the other day he graced mosquitoes and said, "A righteous man regardeth the life of his beast". Thereafter, they both lived happily. A story of false dichotomy and fatal grace! I can fabricate this for as long as I want.

Audin was lying on a rope-cot sagging down in the middle as if the ropes had never been trained for holding a man of such alien psyche. He turned his head towards Rama, rolled in a quilt peacefully on the adjacent cot. "Rama, what would you do if you've been detected of malaria?"

"Why? Why would I?" Having caught some cold already, he spoke in an adenoidal tone.

"Supposing, you have?"

"Get some quinine." He wiped the snot out of his nose which was waiting for the quinine-advice to turn into a reality.

"No, there is a trap. This time the mosquito is graced by the God. Aren't you sure to die a terrible death?"

"I don't know! If that man, I mean..." he sneezed, "...the mosquito is graced, he speaks our languages too. Better ask him, let me die!"

"It occurs to me, sometimes, that you guys, the theistic fraternity, would do great good to the world if you leave creativity to artists, eh, Rama?"

"Isn't it otherwise? It is *we* who are artists!" another sneeze.

Audin's eyes were in line with his feet, and could see the entire street plain and exposed in front, under the sky laden with the collection of stars that had been more appealing than the ceiling in the Nirvana designed by an Italian. Down the street he looked, and kept doing so in a manner of keenness to settle in obviousness.

I must admit the harmless disposition of every bit of this village. I am not able to fit those broken pieces of Delhi nights anywhere, those fancy façades, those long cars, that whistling guard. This simplicity is going to haunt me forever. Something that can be as influential as to haunt someone should also satisfy the primary condition of being one of the most extreme aspects of life- either absolute truth or absolute illusion. Which one of these? The swami looks way more contended with whatever he has been domesticating in his mind and character than me, but how does it all come to the fore? How could such a transparent life accommodate a very opaque, vague character of the God? Where there is a fruitful action, there is a driving force. But where the seed of this driving force is I have to figure out.

Audin kept on speculating about every this and that, and soon fell thoughtless, and slipped into a cheerful sleep, perhaps his first and last. His paraphernalia, including the suitcase that secured the metallic book, was strewn below his cot unattended and carefree, as himself, in a place of unrestricted access.

Filtering in and out the happenings of the day, in no specific order, Audin churned out a number of dreams and the latest was:

A herd of undirected children rushing into the ashram running over one another, some of them hit the hand-pump and decided not to get up, some others ducked down to explore what lied under his cot, some climbed up the guava tree and fell down when the branches came off, on their backs supported by bags, and a few who were more agile reached the roof top. But there was one thing that each of them had in common; they were all bald and had faces similar to that of the Swami except a beautiful girl in an orange frock, appearing to be older than all of them, who came at last and stood beside Audin, while he wasn't awake, and started gently stroking his hair in rhythm with the song that she sang ...India, India, take me to your heart...reveal your ancient mysteries to me...I am searching for an answer...but somewhere deep inside...I know I'll never find it here... it is already in my mind...I've got to follow my heart wherever it takes me...I've got to follow my heart wherever it calls to me. The song was then chanted by every child. The girl picks up the suitcase and prepares to leave. The children, who were busy with their props, aligned themselves around his cot, and stopped singing abruptly. The place is deserted again.

Sharp sunrays were goading Audin's eyelids. As a natural stimulus, he sat himself up. He was bathing in sunlight, alone; the fellow cots had been removed as if the director at a movie set had called off the day. He lowered his hands to touch the presence of the suitcase, which had remained situated obediently there under the latticed shade. The rooms were teeming with children.

Dreams! Huh! It was everywhere. Bald kids, that girl. Whatever it was, it was just a mix up, of that polio picture; I remember revising that song before sleeping. I know it happens.

"There is some water; you can take a bath. It is already late." Rama was towelling his head.

"There? There. At the drain? " Audin wanted to share his dream but resisted.

"... Make it quick or you will miss the breakfast. And the water's not warm."

The scenery around Audin had the diverseness of a theatre room where a play had just ended and lights were switched on. And that idea of Rama's of bathing in this open theatre, where the audience of children and some passers-by without tickets was focused on his every move, was unaffordable to him, and he quit.

"No, I will go for a walk first. Where is everybody?"

"I have not seen Jhelum yet, and Rishi Ji is meditating. So, after that he'll take a yoga class; he is going to see us in the afternoon. Don't go too far, else don't come back hungry."

Audin left for the streets barefooted, glancing over the unseen faces with an enthusiasm that, in the most optimistic state of vision, may have helped him find that beautiful girl in the orange frock and her army somewhere; but he instead got surrounded by mobs of surprised villagers at every turn, left or right, for, they had only heard and not seen ever before a White; there had although been a few untreated Vitiligo patients in the village. Audin, now a morning scandal, was mesmerized by the candour beauty of everything that existed around him as if everything was a part of a poem about 'Randomness'. He went on marching, particularly liking the curvy streets; some of which were extremely wide, apparently compensating for the extremely narrower ones. There was one more warm thing that caught his 'to-let' attention, handmade earthen stoves, placed by the root of every threshold outside the house. This also reminded him of the probable breakfast at the ashram, which he was to let go of for he had already found something more filling.

After spending an hour hitch-hiking, he reached the periphery of Chindauli where the population was comparatively less; the fields were laid till the horizon- as if a painter who had just learnt to draw only green fields lost his sight, and thereafter never drew anything but fields. How 'filling' it must have been!

Audin was impressed. His muddy feet looked like ankle bracelets of elephant skin, perhaps he had been making musical pieces out of everything he saw.

Wearing a white vest, that revealed his hairy body, a young lad was sitting on a wooden chair. The ankle bracelets got pulled towards the new stranger, the magnetic specimen, the intriguing specimen; Audin wanted to have a closer look, or may be a disguised chat.

A mirror hung on the tree trunk. He was trying to align it to its best possible position that could capture a complete visage.

A narcissist who stares at his reflection all day, in a sycophant mirror, to praise the beauty of himself.

As he stretched himself up and down, sometimes on a toe or the heel, or as he twisted himself about his waist, sometimes gripping the chair or the tree, he looked like a black and white dice in motion – shabby and clean at the same time.

Before Audin could make up his mind, the lad saw him nearing, and called out, loudly, "Sir! Sir! Welcome! India! Barber!" He animated his fingers to mime a scissor. "Welcome!"He now scratched his armpits that were seriously damp.

"Ah! Thank you..."Audin settled down on the troubled seat, he already had a few queries in waiting about barbering that were ignored by Rama last night, "...and we can talk in the local language; I understand it, some part of it, most of it."

"Where are you from, Sir?" he came in expertly in the regional Hindi, as if he had matured at least by ten years in a matter of seconds.

"I am from Delhi; been staying there for twenty years."

"Oh! I... I thought you are...a tourist; I have seen lots of them coming to Delhi. So, why have you come here?" he asked with the confidence of an assertive counsellor.

"I have come to meet the Rishi, Jatharu Rishi. I am a friend of Jhelum's husband. Do you know her?"

"Yes, Sir. I am the family barber, Ghaal. They would have told you, Sir. Would you like to have a shave, Sir?" Audin thought of Jhelum's family as the monarchs who had a personal, owned barber to whom they donated a piece of land to work in his spare time.

"Shave, and a haircut. You are their personal barber?"

"Not just one, Sir, to many, and there are three barber families in Chindauli. We handle most of the work, Sir. I am familiar with everything, about barbering work, Sir. I am in total control of this shop."

Ghaal was lying; the whole set up of the makeshift shop depended on the control of the tree's trunk. A wooden tray affixed to it, of the colour and shape of the lower jaw of an ape who had plaque deposits, held all the professional equipment – a scissor, a tumbler, a rubber case, and a towel.

Having wiped a razor off with a soggy newspaper a couple of times, he looked at his poker face customer, and made a few more diligent attempts at wiping as he wasn't sure of what a clean blade should look like. He at last made the first stroke. Audin could sense, with his neck lying askew, the cold, sharp edge rubbing against his skin, and, penetrating his thoughts; the blade with its repetitive strokes was behaving like a fink who desperately wanted to whisper the secret hint- *'Every child of your dream got shaved here, right here.'*

He exhaled voluntarily to concentrate on Ghaal.

"Are you making a...," Ghaal bent Audin's head sideways, "...a film on Rishi Ji?" now talking to Audin's chin.

Audin, surprised, started a countdown to cross out everything that made him look like a film maker or even a prop-maker. He shrugged off the accusation, and suggested that Ghaal was a better actor than barber.

"So, you said you are a personal barber...do barbers also lift luggage in this village?"

"Yes, Sir, it is a custom. Barbers are errands, and do many other services; sometimes lifting luggage too. It is our living. Barbering doesn't fetch enough money."

"Alright, so, is this your own shop, or an inheritance?"

"Both."

"And since when have you been handling it?"

"I inherited it after my father's death. I was the only son. I have been here since I was ten. "

"...and Jatharu Rishi?"

"Rishi ji has not come to my shop anytime."

"No, I mean, for how long has he been living in this village?"

"Rishi ji? Sir, he is from the era of my grandfathers." He laughed to hide a smirk. A good actor he was.

"What does he do for a living; like you work as a barber?"

"You are *English*, sir; you won't understand. He is the Guru. What does he need to do? Nothing, Sir, nothing. It's his mercy that Chindauli has flourished, he is the lifeline." The word "English" was louder than other weak lumps of alphabets; it only meant that Audin must not feel offended if Ghaal preserves his 'English' hair for a lifetime.

"Flourished? Will you elaborate on that? 'Chindauli has flourished'."

"What is to elaborate, Sir? It is women who elaborate, men don't. Yes, but, my father used to say that no one dies an untimely death in our village. It is true." This reminded Audin of what his father told him in the diary.

The keeper of the metallic book died an untimely death.
Now I, the keeper, am in a village where no one dies untimely. Beauty of mythology!

"There is no one who doesn't bow down to him, Sir. No one!"

"And you?" The question arrested the momentum of his scissor. Ghaal answered stubbornly, as if defending himself for a crime he did not commit, "Yes! Why not! He is God to me, to all of us."

"...but, he is a human after all. You know that."Audin answered with purposed innocence.

"Why do you bother to meet him then? You have travelled such a long distance."

Why do I bother to meet him?
Indeed, I have travelled miles. It matters little, not at all, if I do this a million light years away or under my nose. It's a choice, whichever is more becoming. One doesn't steal cookies from his own jar. It's his jar, he just takes it. I cannot be criticised for going far afield, this isn't criticism- it's beguilement- an invalid form of defence to steer the opponent away from conclusion. But there is one thing that's holing me- Overthinking. Overthinking seems like a psychological tax, or a debt, for having thought about anything heard, seen or read. The theist doesn't

bother about paying the tax at all. Can I ever become as
carefree as this barber?

"...and Swami ji? Where has he come from? Is
he as carefree as you?" Audin made Ghaal's last
question go astray after being run off in the surge of
disconnected thoughts.

"Swami ji? He is the son of the priest of the
Shiva temple. Got influenced by Rishi ji so much
that he abandoned his household life, family..." The
barber had started massaging his head; a soothing
jingle at this minute would have lifted him off the
seat.

"How do you like my massaging, Sir?"

"It's good. If there is one thing that can personify
brainwashing, it's massaging."

"I knew you would say something good about it,
Sir."

"So, where does his family live now? A little slower...
to the left...."

The vapours of sunflower oil were afloat with a new
identity – fragrance. The thin fragrance. The oil had
been prepared in the morning, and still carried the
middle name 'Warm'.

"The same place. He has a younger brother staying
with his parents, but Swami Ji's wife re-married.
Though he had already become a Brahmchari."

"What is that? *Brahmchari?*" Audin wanted to know,
under his English cloak, if his specimen's knowledge
was hearsay or acquired.

"They do not associate with women; even while talking to them they are very cautious. You need not worry, Sir, English people keep so many wives."

"What? Where have you heard that from?" Audin smiled, and kept smiling as if he was hearing with his mouth.

"I have watched English films; I do whenever I go to Delhi."

"That is very untrue, Ghaal. Will you ever go to England? You know so much about it."

"If destiny wants, and God is willing, maybe I will set up a shop there. I would want name it 'Chindauli'." And he had touched the raw nerve.

A balancer, a mosquito charmer, and now a flight captain, the God seems to be a bottle of panacea lying in a dustbin.

"So, Ghaal, if someone who has no legitimate connection with the God, what should he do to go to England?"

"Is there anyone like that? No one, Sir." This was a very simplistic reply, as simplistic as a slap.

"You are so pristine in your words, your behaviour. You never think that you are missing the real part of this world, beyond this, that you have never seen before?"

"Do you mean I should get married?"

The barber had never speculated the other way; he was a time-tested believer.

"Ghaal, have you ever walked over a dirty doormat?"

"No, Sir..."

"...Sir, I think you must see Rishi ji soon, before villagers accuse me for your madness."

"I aspire for that. It is only madness that challenges intelligence, in the face, it is that powerful. We should all educate ourselves to be mad."

"Look!"

"What?"

"She is here!"

"Who?"

Ghaal distanced himself from Audin, "The mad woman."

"Get on Audin!" she pierced her throat out.

"Huh?" The blaring horn of the thundering tractor dragged Audin out of the thinking tank.

"Jhelum? I am, I was just, yes, I was about to come..." Audin groped himself for the wallet foolishly, as if he had been wearing someone else's clothes, and handed Ghaal a five hundred rupee note in a complacency that expected no change in return whatsoever.

The wheels wished to trundle, only trundle, until she overlooked their existence and the tractor caromed off every corner. Menace! Menace had been her trail! The bandwagon eventually stopped at the ashram; she rammed it through the entrance. Audin dismounted, his skin was nostalgically throbbing as if he had ridden the combustion engine itself.

I thought it had square wheels.

Another man, bald, shaven eyebrows, was locked in a yoga asana. He was double aged- a plain face enwrapping more than fifty years of past, and a thin casing of a Korean teenager. Rama, sitting beside him in the same posture, had been holding his breath to limits. He spat first, no, he spoke first, no, perhaps he lost control over his tongue and everything floating around it, "He, is, Au..., Audin, S, Stewart!" and collapsed in a cough that kept echoing.

This man, Jatharu Rishi, lacked curiosity, but his expressions were swollen of wisdom as if there was nothing left to be explored. Having performed the asana, he took some time to stand up, allowing Audin to wonder about his muscular flexibility.

"You are a yoga master. I have, personally, never met a traditional yogi." Audin began the talk unconventionally.

"Yoga is union with God; it is the life." Audin heard for the first time the voice whose words he had been hearing for years. The voice was quick, in a vague hurry, and apparently egotistical.

"How is it 'union with God', Rishi ji, if I can call you that...?"

He did not reply. He was hard of hearing on unwanted questions. "How is it union...Is it a simulation of Hindu deities? Is that...what you meant?"

"Huh? Did you say something?"

"I asked how it is 'union with God'; is it another self-explanatory hypothesis on finding the God with-in, or no more than a way of physical betterment?"

"Then, then you are an idiot. Not accepting a thing until you know it is inquisitiveness, and rejecting it without knowing is foolishness." The intelligence had made his egotism appear subdued aggression, or, more euphemistically, earthy rudeness to Audin.

"I have no disagreement with the first part. Your diction suggests that you strongly believe you are qualified enough to judge. What is the reason for that?"

"Reason for?"

"...for concluding that I am an idiot when I disagree with you. You may infer, though."

"I am qualified by my master; I am the knower of the absolute source of wisdom-- the Vedas, revealed by God himself. That won't appeal to you. I have a doctorate in Hindu philosophy. Does it make you a better idiot?"

"I will need time to get accustomed to your way of demanding answers."

Jatharu smiled, floutingly, with an aristocratic confidence that could make anyone believe that his intelligence was always out of reach. He was always at a distance, an unachievable distance, as if he could put a restriction on how fast one can think, process his words- a distance of closest approach. Swami came in swiftly and unlocked the first room, the outer one alongside the entrance; Jatharu may have cued him to do so, however, nobody could notice any exchange of this action-reaction between the two.

Jatharu's ashram was an unusual place- like those that are equally suitable for animals as well as humans- where any room that has served its purpose is immediately shut, as if to build some artificial feeling of confinement.

The smell of the room was not entirely nauseating, but there had been something missing from there. A dry sponge would explain it, a dry sponge that has been lying on a rooftop for years- if you can smell those tiny pores those are Jatharu's rooms.

The space had been least pretentious, and most empty; a woven mat, and a large framed portrait, colourless, of yet another bald man sitting in the lotus posture; the liveliness of his eyes was haunting as if he could influence your views about the bad and the good. But he did not look harmful. He was a pair of sunken, vague eyes that can follow you uninvited, to whisper in your ears, only whisper, about whatever ill you have done in your life, and silently disappear. The only purpose of this room seemed to entertain this man when he secretly descends from the frame after midnight.

Audin, curious and opinionated, got his vision snared by the edges of the frame, and the dark contours of its dweller. He was stuck, "Is he your father? I see very similar mannerisms, a first impression."

"Foster father. He is my master. He made me what I am today."

"So, I mean, what is the need of a master? You said the knowledge you have has been revealed to you by the God himself? I am trying to boil it down to that point, because you are, you are contradicting yourself, frankly."

"Being foolish is not as harmful as enjoying being foolish. You enjoy asking foolish questions. Do you want me to reply?"

"Yes." Audin had never been afraid of baseless humiliation.

"It leaves no scope of speculation. If there is no master people try to learn on their own, try to find a cause of mysteries that are beyond their scope, and waste their lives. Sometimes, by his mercy or what you call 'accident,' they discover something that is already kept in place by God himself - they call it their own invention. Invention is a myth. Just like when you start treading on an untouched path, you keep treading on it, keep treading on it for days, the sand, the grass gets flattened, and finally you say that you have created a new path. That's not a new path, it existed even before you, the fool, you were born. A master is needed so that you don't mix your own ideas with the absolute truth. Haven't you seen this? You think you are a good observer; haven't you?"

"Well, that's called experimentation. People lay down 'laws' on basis of experimentation, and experimentation doesn't need to be guided by a 'master.' What is wrong? Why does experimentation not sound right?"

"There is an acid, hydrochloric acid. Tasted it? What is the colour? Of hydrochloric acid."

Rama was so bored of the talks that he had been relating every discoloured patch on the wall with the faces he had ever known. Audin, in these times of scientific enquiries, played dead; he was waiting for him to become his council.

"...it is transparent, colourless," Rama promptly replied shifting his focus away from his workbook as soon as he felt two faces, present in the room, demanding immediate attention from him.

"So...a child says that he wants to put his finger into the beaker of the acid to test what it is. The master says, 'No, you must not; it will hurt your finger badly... it is acidic.' The child says "I am curious; let me experiment; it is water, I have seen water hundred times; I am wise." Then, he puts the finger in, and cries out. So, what do you say? Was he wise enough?"

"He was desperately curious."

"No, no, he was an idiot like you. Tell me, you burn your finger, cry out, and then reach a conclusion that 'Oh...yes it is acid' instead of reaching the same conclusion without losing your finger by accepting what your master said. You see, people, people dovetail God as per their needs- mix their own ideas, corrupt everything. I haven't met one atheist who has read scriptures, who has given up on God after understanding scriptures. No one! They go on speculating on their own, like a part-time service, without any master, and then shout loud, "Look! We haven't found anything! Hence, there is no God. So, which one is wiser? Or better? Experimentation or accepting the established fact...? Tell me?"

"That, experimentation..., provided him more satisfaction."

"That is false satisfaction. It is only a feeble sense of satisfaction, because you have hurt your finger; you will not be able to forget it throughout your life; that makes you proud of your effort and feel satisfied. It is all false. People like you encourage such tactics. Sometimes they don't even reach a conclusion and keep losing their fingers one by one, and call it satisfaction. Satisfaction is the only solution, I tell you, but you should not go after temporary satisfaction."

"So, a master is the only way to the solution, the non-temporary satisfaction, as per you? I strongly disagree."

"Oh! Your disagreement, or agreement, holds no merit. You accept science to be aid of everything, you surrender unto science. Better to get rid of science too, no aid at all!"

"I am not a science aspirant. I do not advocate for science either. I am an uninfluenced atheist."

"Rama has a scientific temperament, but he knows that science is a dog's bone. It requires basic intelligence to understand God, God doesn't want noble laureates. These are basically two different spheres- God's intelligence is limitless, let's call it infinity, your intelligence is a tiny freckle that dies out in less than hundred years. So, a tiny freckle cannot understand infinity on its own. If it does, then, we can undoubtedly conclude that, that tiny freckle's intelligence is at least equal to God's intelligence, equal to infinity, if not more, uh? You understand? So, actually the tiny freckle has become infinity, you see? So, basically, you either become one with God to understand him, or you fall in love with him and he reveals himself. The first approach is very impersonal, the second is personified, but both the approaches require God's own will, his agreement. Science doesn't fit anywhere. Now, you, the atheist, the rascal, you say that with your tiny freckle intelligence you reject God! I pity you."

"I usually don't use science to defend myself. Science is not the supreme authority."

"Then who is the third party? You killed Science, you killed God, who is the third party?"

"Chance. Things may happen without triggering other events, that's what I believe in. There need not be a cause-effect relationship. It's a faulty mind-set to put everything in cause-effect mould, there may or may not be a cause-effect thing, it is just a matter of chance."

"You are making things difficult for you. No 'cause-effect' is another impersonal definition of God, which means you have faith in one of the features of God. He has no cause-effect ideology, and at the same time can trigger innumerable events without being the cause. You are, you are just an impatient seed of theism waiting for the first rains."

"As I said, what I meant was effect does not prove the existence of cause. Causeless-ness is not equal to Effectless-ness or vice versa. It's a very simple theory- I may be a no cause-effect entity and still trigger events just by chance, that doesn't justify that I have become God. That's what I am trying to say, Rishi Ji, that 'Chance' has its own identity, 'Chance' can do anything. If you say that God became God by chance, I am ready to accept God as a product of a chance."

"You just gave another rascaldom, God is not an outcome of a cause-effect event. What triggered that cause, by the way, which generated God? "

"Chance. Now, I don't need to wonder about God's supremacy, Chance may generate another God. The word 'God' is just a catchy name."

"Chance is your God?"

"Not at all, Rishi Ji. I don't have to personify Chance. It's not the demigod Chance. It's not the Mr Chance. It's a thoughtless entity. Just as some scientists used to say that space is filled with ether, everything that can or cannot be observed is filled with 'Chance.' It has the most neutral existence."

"Chance! Experimentation! Everything born out of this autodidactic way of life! Anyways, leave it if you cannot help. Rama said you have a Sanskrit book, you need my help. I don't want to be aggressive, come to the point."

The suitcase, which had been a sensitive theme of his dream last night, was opened.

"It is, uh, not a book perhaps. I would call it my ancestral property. My father revealed about it a day before he died. This is why I have come here, to do what he said."

"Oh! Very nice it is, very attractive, but...but, one must not have so much attachment to material possessions, however much expensive it is."

"I don't have attachment to possessions, expensive or cheap, I wanted to only-"

"Only what? Only? Only wanted to deal it for experiments, make me your accomplice? That won't happen."

"Uh, no, you mistook me. Actually, my father wrote a letter to me, in his diary, the final letter; he said this book has mystic powers, and is a source of mysticism. He wanted me to do something about it; so, Rama said I must talk to you."

Jatharu held the metallic book in one hand with his head at a snobbish distance which clearly announced that had Rama not been a reference here he would not have even put his sacred gaze on it; but soon the distance contracted, and he had to place the book right below his eyes; the book could not be read at other angles.

"From where...uh, who gave it you?" There was composure in his voice, evocative of a corroded glass turning silver again, telling him to behave respectably in front of the guest.

"What is your name? Audin...?"

"Audin, Stewart."

"No! It's not here." Hearing the name, he closed the book at once in immense satisfaction which got spilled when he shut his eyes fugitively.

"What? Do you see something interesting?"

Jatharu left the room in his trademark pace and closed himself in the sacristy; following which, Swami, who was busy preparing for the evening chores, dashed himself in.

"I saw him running? Rama?" Without exploring the answer, he turned back towards the meshed window to peep in, covering it dutifully like a curtain, he said overwhelmingly, "Rishi ji?"

"Yes. Don't come in. I don't want anyone to come in. Is this sentence so ambiguous? Don't come in!"

"The cupboard is open. He is reading a book. Rama, what happened?" Swami became too watchful, as if he had been pick-pocketed and wanted to go back in time to locate evidence.

The sudden upsurge of concern in Jatharu's conduct was apparently substantiating the claims of Mr Sayiid.

Swami was to have lost his composure, but he bartered a few ad hoc ounces of tolerance by investigating Audin for the next two hours. They both were simply interviewing each other with no intervention.

"I have never seen him like this; he is always so prudent and contended." As Swami spoke of his master he could not miss overlooking the discrepancy in his yesterday's and today's self.

The sacristy stored variety of Indian scriptures, and other rare pieces of writings. This was the Rishi's personal collection of spirituality, a spiritual kaleidoscope, built over a period of several decades. An aged collection of unbound papers, the Rig Veda, was supposed to lead him into this research- the Rig Veda reveals explicitly about the cosmic manifestation, and the world's origin. Jatharu was wildly chasing some 'text', he remembered skimming through it once when he had been a passionate student. The fluttering of pages seemed so irrelevant; Jatharu was fidgeting, his fingers shouting, almost criticising someone who was standing in the doorway to heavens.

"O my omniscient master!" He found it, and then lit a candle for the sharp light needed in the claustrophobic room never meant for reading. He chanted the text repeatedly, to confirm its existence, and then chanted its meaning, repeatedly, to appreciate his own faculty to reacquaint.

"The ether that has held this universe in its plane and the planets in their orbits, that ether condenses into the form of shining leaves on which are inscribed the arrows of the quiver of the Apaursheya's. The leaves can never be destroyed by a weapon, can never be melted by fire, can never be macerated by water, and can never be decomposed by earth; like a soul that is never born and is eternal."

The identification marks that were mentioned in the text matched verbatim; not ready to digest the truth he continued till his throat went husky. There emerged no way which could have compensated for the ease with which he had ridiculed Audin.

This is not possible. Audin is a thug. What does my master want me to do?

"Rishikesh? Give me some water!" Swami handed him a glass of water manoeuvring his hand through the window bars behind which was the prisoner of his own wits.

The successor of the world! Let it happen, I would just let it happen to me. I must coax this thug into renouncing this godsend present or must I not?

The natural light was fading every minute. The dusk chanced upon Chindauli and passed away too soon. The cupboard, the walls, and other scattered paraphernalia of worship ceremonies were veneered by darkness. He was contemplating all alone on this Earth, as if writing the final conclusion of the book of humanity for generations to come. The glare of the melting candle, the golden leaves, and his oscillating shadow were piercing through his mind, as if it were a council of war to stop Jatharu, to order him to hold back his deceitful ideas, to object his conceit before it outruns his very wisdom. Staring at nothing explicable, he went into a bitter state of strain and blew the candle out. He was effusing sweat.

Inescapable dilemma, Oh my master! Inescapable dilemma! I feel estranged. Lend me your spiritual eyes to find the righteous side. Is it the time for me to become the successor of this world? For all the selfless service that I have offered to you, for the celibate life I have lived, for the philanthropy I have practiced, for your message that I have preached? Am I faultless in accepting the leaves as your command, and proceed? Does everything belong to this man who doesn't not belong to this holy land of Sages? How would he who looks down upon the creator handle the creation? You have made me the churning rope binding the 'Mandarachala' hill, I cannot sustain this pull.

He crossed his legs to sit in the lotus posture before intonating the sound of '*Om*'. He breathed in, and got ruffled by the pungent smell of that snuffed wick. Nothing seemed easy all of a sudden; having broken his rhythm he stood up and "trespassed" the door.

"I will bathe!" Jatharu pointed to Swami who had dichotomized his senses, one affixed on the door, the other listening to Audin, and the rest had run out of business. Whatever the master ordered was obeyed to the importance of a tenet. Jatharu poured the water haphazardly on his bald head, purifying himself with its transparency and coldness, besides gargling the hymns.

"You are not aware of what you have...This man, Audin, does not know what he has brought...." He began talking to all of them after feeling collected, and settled down on the mat he had left without saying much in the afternoon.

"I have a little idea of what I have." Audin replied attentively.

"These are wisdom leaves. Wisdom leaves. They are not made of any earthy element."

"I would agree to that; this is a report by a scientist who has-"

"I need no proofs! Vedas are the proof. How did your father- no! Put it back..."Jatharu asked Audin to let the report be in the suitcase forever, "How could your father have these?"

"He left me a diary, whatever I know is whatever he wanted me to know. Whatever I tell is an interpretation of his final letter."

"What all did he tell?"

"Aurangzeb had gotten this book from a Hindu saint, whom he buried in one of the walls of the fort, the Jahgarh fort. Then, presented this to one of my ancestors, Sir James Stewart. Thus, it...has been descending for ages in our lineage."

"See, this is what I fail to understand! No one can accept this statement. How can one accept this? That, this, that, uh, these wisdom leave got snatched away by a king. This doesn't even make for folklore. But this man has the wisdom leaves, Rishikesh, and he is not the Apaursheya..," Jatharu himself was keen to snatch away the wisdom leaves, and to send the thug back to his infancy, but only by playing under the pretence of a morally correct seizure; the most appropriate of all would have been to take birth in the Stewart lineage, "You don't know the literal meaning, how can you become the successor?"

"Successor?"

"We need to discuss this, I'll tell you."

"The successor, the Apaursheya, is the controller of the world on behalf of God himself. He is the owner of all the mystic powers. That is it. I cannot explain more. It is beyond your scope of speculation."

"Well, that is what 'I' cannot accept so flawlessly. My father held similar views but I would not hesitate to say..."

"Wait! You don't have to accept things as they are. You have to accept things for the sake of Chance! Sounds better? Chance brought mystic powers, this is 'mysticism by chance', do you get it clever boy?"

"Yes, but it is the identity of Chance that doesn't allow..."

"No, Stop that. It's not going anywhere. I don't want to watch the cause-effect puppetry again. Why don't you just listen to what I am telling you, why is that so difficult?"

"Yes, Rishi ji."

"So, so, I was going to tell you, that, yes...that you can reduce your body to the size of a grain; you can expand your body to the size of the universe; you can transfer your body to any place known or unknown; thousands of such powers...One can possess all these powers by rightly pursuing the wisdom leaves."

Rama rarely argued with Jatharu- whatever the Rishi said was more factual than the rising of the sun. The glories of the Apaursheya rejuvenated the sparkle of life in Rama's heart, he could have illustrated his exuberance with an incurable rush of tears had the master been a little more melodious in his words.

"I have not a speck of doubt that you are the successor." Hearing this overwhelming statement, Audin and Jatharu, both did not react.

Rama stooped down to touch Jatharu's feet, and asked his friend to do the same. Audin, under normal circumstances of a casual meet, would have followed Rama in what he considered a mockery, but Rama started to repeat the sport back and forth so much so that it looked like a one-man procession.

"This is absolutely against the laws of nature." Audin continued.

"That is because you are not aware of what power means. You know that? Who is the most powerful? Most powerful man that you know?"

"It solely depends on the context...May I know? The context?"

"So, you say, you cannot generalise? You need a context?"

Audin looked around the room, expecting to see something that may help him exemplify his answer, and found the waiting eyes in the portrait; he could have awarded them of being the most powerful, but went for the experiences with specimens and said, "Generalisation is, I believe, the core of many philosophical theories; it has never been easy...for me...It is never; the context is needed."

"...Don't worry; I will try to make it contextual for you, Audin." Jatharu said, emphasising the "you" too much.

"A grasshopper is eating some grass peacefully. A frog passes by and plunges upon him and the grasshopper becomes the food. Then, a snake, noticing this activity, surreptitiously creeps up to the same frog, eats him. Now, an eagle hovering above comes rushing downwards and crumbles the snake into pieces for his lunch. The eagle gradually loses health and dies, and again some grass grows out of its decomposed carcass which feeds another grasshopper to continue the cycle. So, tell me who was the most powerful of them all?"

"Give me some time."

"Cannot you generalise out of it something? It is an elementary food chain? I have provided you the context."

"Death? That power cannot resist death."

"Uh, no! I reject that. It is the fact that there is nobody in this world who is most powerful; everybody is relatively powerful, applicable to every species. No one can exercise his powers independently! There is no one, not a single soul, who can be independently powerful. Is it so complex a generalisation?"

"Is that a valid generalisation?" The obviousness of the generalisation raised desperate doubts in Audin's mind.

"You can test. Experiment! I have left that scope. I always do. Anyways, how could it be invalid? You seemed to have said that succumbing to your ability of opposing everything, anything; opposing everything is so depressing. I think you couldn't find that generalisation on your own? I don't mind your opposition. Do you have any exception?"

Audin, in the same posture, fumbled, upturned, and magnified several pictures in the trunks of his mind, and created many such cycles in the air but none of them defied the quoted generalisation.

"Why don't you tell me if you have an exception?"

"I will."

"No, you have to tell me now, Audin, otherwise you would start afresh with that rascaldom of Chances."

"...I don't have any exception right now but..."

"...and do you have an exception?" Jatharu asked Rama, who had been holding his hands in leak-proof obedience, and had begun planning for his life of seclusion with his master, who he thought had been disguising himself in this mortal form until now but was the Apaursheya himself.

"No, Rishi ji, I have no arguments left."

"The Apaursheya, thus, is the only independently powerful personality. Not dependent on any worldly man, but God. Apaursheya is the sole controller of his powers and other's. Apaursheya can, if he wants, evaporate all the oceans. Apaursheya can hollow out this Earth from its centre. Apaursheya is the knower of all hidden truths. These wisdom leaves have descended from Lord Brahma himself, passing from all the demi-gods. Apaursheya thus can control the flow of air, water etc.; everything that is controlled otherwise by demigods, or the controller of individual powers. Apaursheya is the supreme." Rama's ears had transformed into tulips, and whenever the word "Apaursheya" was called, he heard his master's name. Audin, on the other side, had grown a sieve on his ears barring him from making any mental picture.

"This is then the only exception to your generalisation? The Apaursheya who is independent?"

Jatharu expanded his insidious desires into laughter, "You, so, you," he laughed again, "you are not going to accept him as the representation of God, or even a superhuman, but as a mere exception. That needs a stone bent of mind." Audin agreed as a matter of fact, he had not given up on fighting back but on fighting back hard. A parasite was invading him- the 'void' developed by the generalisation theory; something like this had not happened in a long time.

"...Anyways, I need an hour's sleep." Jatharu asked them to leave the room.

Audin went near the Guava tree to feel its companionship. He often used to tell Bhola Prasad when the latter was busy cutting espaliers of the Northern Ridge, *"A tree at a dead end is a bridge to the other side of yours and you."* Only a day had passed, and whosoever was there around him was a resident of a distant planet where everybody behaved in a manner very different from his, this had exhausted him from all dimensions. Rubbing his palms on its bark, he looked at Rama, who was counting the blades of grass, with his mouth open, he had plucked in the last fifteen minutes, "What are you going to do after returning to Delhi? Are you missing something?"

"Why? No, we just came yesterday. You are probably homesick. It is a good place."

"Yes, people, here, are good. I don't know, not homesick. It's a different way altogether." He only remembered Ghaal at this point of time who, though amiable, belonged to the same planet.

"What way? I think you are tired; even I am. And this change of food, and water; we have been put on fruits." He said casually.

"You are right; I shall rest."

He fell on the cot, and began to crack the knuckles of his fingers, and then his toes. Tonight's pattern of stars was no different from the previous night except they were communicative to Audin. He could see an audience in them like he had seen in his seminars; they were waiting for an elocutionary explanation to the questions that had been hurled at him. He remained studded there, in an embarrassed silence, as if he had blanked out on a dais; and gradually turned away his sight to the mysterious room of the leader of the opposition- the turbulence behind the walls was not yet subdued; Jatharu had resolved many such cases before- he was an acclaimed astrologer, a mathematician, and an Ayurvedic healer.

The door, ajar, got opened with untamed suddenness; Jatharu came out holding a piece of paper. Swami at this instant perceived this as an obligation calling him to come down from the roof.

"I have calculated when the reign ends! The calculations are accurate! You will find it very interesting, it is not a coincidence!"Audin braced himself for what was being called interesting.

"The constellation is approaching in a month, twenty eight days; you can oblige the demi-gods of constellations, and become the Apaursheya!"

"Gods of constellations?"

"No! You see these hemispheres? They are the planets; they form a constellation. Every constellation has a mystic power; if you satisfy the owner of the constellation, you can procure it! It is not very difficult." The hemispheres had been debated about often. Audin could recollect Dr Sayiid's indications about a planetary system, and that he had stranded the scientist who might have handed him a better finding than Jatharu.

"We are left with twenty eight days!" Jatharu was darting information all across the ashram.

"Rishi ji, I told you, that I certainly need some time to get accustomed to your way of demanding answers. I can't say anything else; I think we should continue tomorrow, shouldn't we?"

"You don't have to say; listen to what I am saying. You don't have sufficient knowledge; you may not have your say all the time. If you can annihilate the bones and offer the ashes on the day of this constellation...it is all yours...I shall guide you. I shall guide you!"

"Bones! Whose bones are being talked about? Rama! I am shall not participate in any, any pyric ritual."

"The last successor's! His bones...they never decompose, until they get the five elements- earth, air, fire, water, ether. It is a scared process, not a tantric...

"I am afraid, whatever is that you will have to do on your own."

"Why?"

"...because I do not want any powers, I have no desire to become the successor. There is no reason for me not to stay out of this." Audin expressed his views quite unrelated to what Jatharu had planned.

"Then why do you not let me become!" Jatharu shouted, releasing the pent up slurry of disgust. Swami wanted to confront Audin, he was already accusing him, in his mind, of the blasphemy Audin had just committed by disobeying him. Rama nodded at Audin to stay unmoved till he intervenes as if revering the master's obstinacy was a founding pillar of one's quest for absolute truth, but Audin was naturally unaffected, "Rishi ji, I never intended to be an obstruction. I do not understand how I am being an obstruction, perhaps I have not been able to make you..."

"No...No....It is alright, I am alright... I got furious; it's...just...ah..." Jatharu had, in those few minutes of subsiding infuriation, chalked out another plan, and he again went by the same coated tone that requested to erase from their memories what had just happened. "...Look... I know you will not want powers, but undoubtedly there is much more for you. See, if I get the powers, it will only prove the existence of the supernatural. Would you not like to witness that, something that will challenge your philosophies and prove mine? And, more importantly, you would agree to it that, that, if I become the successor you will liberate the burden of solving this mystery of wisdom leaves, the plates, means your filial duty accomplished! Everything accomplished! That is why I shouted... That is why...because you were reluctant...A sage like me always wants to benefit the people around him." There was conviction in the plan, backed by the passionate desire to become the successor. It had been mixed with the ingredients matching Audin's taste. The subtlety in Jatharu's words had intruded Audin's sieve. "I want you to accompany me. Moreover, it is not a ritual, it's an experiment. You will annihilate the bones, because you have brought the fifth element, the ether. I would like to give you the privilege. You may deny, but that's fine with me, whatever you think of it. Since, I mean, noting that you are a remarkable experimenter, since your coming here is a part of an experiment, you should not hesitate to append this chapter, another chapter to...so as to sum up your experiment. Sounds rational?"

"Partly."

"'Partly', partly would be presumed you are willing, you are open for this?"

"I am open."

We shall leave for the Jahgarh fort tomorrow morning; we will find that wall where the last successor was buried, and annihilate his bones."

"Aren't you running a little too fast? You cannot find a wall in a fort; it is impractical if you don't formulate a plan. The king must have buried thousands of prisoners, at unknown locations. You need a basic lay out for experimentation, even for a pyric ritual."

"It was always a practice to scribe the name of the convicts on the walls who were being buried, much like tombstones. It is not impractical to locate."

"Then, the name? Who will know the name? Someone who got buried around 1700 AD? I would be taken aback if you are about to say that you can, by playing around with astrology, predict the name..."

"It's here." Jatharu looked deep into Audin's eyes to make sure that he was taken aback.

The twenty-eighth plate bore the names of all the predecessors. That was why he was immensely satisfied, for there had been no name called "Audin," when he had been handed the leaves for the first time.

"Anutaapa! The last successor. This is it. Whoever is the new successor, the wisdom leaves will manifest his name. One of us will meet the purpose of his life! You must trust me."

"The plate manifests the name on its own? So, even the manifestation, if I can witness this, would suffice."

Chapter 9

Unfortunate looking bushes dotted the barren lands around the Jahgarh fort perched on the oldest mountains of India, the Aravallies. A kilometre down the hills, the four tourists were measuring the extremities of the front walls that stood high like a file of mammoth biscuits baking under the wide open sun. The noise of heat waves slapping the fort whimsically, as a pride of lions playing with the flesh of a deer, was heard as roars to the ascendants. Hauling against the stubborn winds, and dusting the steep pathway of rocks and thorns, they arrived at one of the entrances of the fort known as the Owaani Gate.

"I need water?" Rama asked to a face, for only the face had been identifiable, sitting in a kiosk which was the ticket office.

"We only sell tickets..." The face looked at his colleague's face, and both burst into a laughter that was made to appear boastful by the solemn and robust bastions of the fort.

"Foreigners one hundred, and for the rest of you, fifty...It is there on the board."

The blue coloured board with misspelled words was used as a legitimate authority to grant Audin the title of being a foreigner and buy him the esteemed entry ticket.

"Whatever you say...and where can we get the water?"

A dwarfish and weak man, showcasing a handlebar moustache, stepped out of the kiosk with a confidence of extracting water out of the dry air by sleight of his venous hands. "I am the registered guide of the fort; I will tour you; only two hundred rupees..."

The world amassed in the womb of the fort; behind the narrow entrance, it was colourful, and vivid, and chaotic, and a negation of the desert. A refreshingly large open space was teeming with tourists. A parade of elephants covered in bright red clothes onto their torso came out from another arched entrance of the opposite complex, with bronze bells hanging around the necks making an ever-lasting clinking sound, accompanied by the blowing of traditional trumpets, and the beating of drums by a group of local musicians wearing enigmatic turbans. On the other side, where stood the small shady trees, an elderly woman was stooping down sweeping the stoned floor, and shooing away the foolish pigeons occasionally with her broom; a few more swept the stairs to a raised platform leading to other entrances. Whiling the duty hours, a pair of jobless looking security men were whistling aimlessly to ensure their own presence.

Bedazzled by the intense activity, like he was one of the myopic patients made to look at a dense source of light very soon after the treatment, Rama said, "Is this a part of the fort? I thought it was an abandoned..."

"This fort is a thousand years old. It is stretched in three kilometres from north to south, and one kilometre from east to west. The veranda you are standing on is called Jeevan Chowk." The confident guide had an ascending-descending way of speaking that was similar to the alternate beating of two hammers on one anvil.

The lofty walls that were made of red sandstone had been a favourite of assorted tourists who were engaged in overusing their cameras in every possible angle and elevation; and with every such tourist accompanied one such man who called himself a registered guide.

This open veranda had two long galleries on both sides, in the form of a museum, which displayed the remnants of the Royal Kingdom- Cannons, guns, pistols, swords, shields, stamps, locks, oil-containers, maps, hand-written books, and photographs of the Kings and their kin.

"So, we are to search a needle in this haystack." Audin couldn't count the number of different sized walls, and thus placed them one over the other loosening his imagination like an infant, and the structure must have touched the moon.

"This place was a barracks for soldiers; before that it was a stable. All these cannons have been manufactured in Jahgarh's own foundry."

Rama had announced, last night, to serve his master for life in sentiment of the revelation and of the triumphant achievement, but the rough estimation of the footwork demanded by the task made him sit on a bench that had not been noticed yet, and ask for a compromising solution.

"It is going to be a little difficult...,"he said in a hushed manner, talking only to Audin.

"On that platform there was a temple which Aurangzeb demolished after capturing the fort." The guide kept elaborating the script as a matter of course as no one listened, for they had been thinking about where to begin, expressing the cluelessness of a naïve mechanic ordered to mend a complex machine; except Jhelum, who was so fascinated by the cannons and the artillery that this reservoir of weapons seemed to her the end of all searches for powers, and she began to explore alone. Audin and Jatharu, like a coin with two vastly distinct faces, appeared superficially paired up for the same cause.

"Please do not, madam! They are royal masterpieces." The guide waved his hand at Jhelum who was rotating the barrel of a small cannon, as if it had been a binocular that needed cleaning. Audin glanced over his suitcase to ascertain it had "his" masterpiece. Intolerable of soliciting at any point of time, she retorted sharply, "Dare not show me that

courage again! You don't weigh more than my arms!"
and the weak man came to notice that her arms had
been strong enough to fling him out of the fort, and
that he was no more than a piece of stone on a
slingshot.

"She is a police woman; need not worry, I assure
you..."Rama made an underhand appeal.

"There is not much we can do; the most basic idea
is to divide. We shall then meet here after an hour."

"Are you to stay more? I have to take you to other
parts as well, if you are..." The threatened guide
requested if the men were interested in him at all.
They were causing unreasonable delay, he thought.
The circumstances were scattered, and he could not
be made a part of the rest of the journey, they thought.

"I have no problem in staying here. But because
you were asking for water, there are many shops
inside the fort, so I thought we could move forward...
It is high noon."

"You stay with her, you can tell her about those
weapons, and meanwhile...we will stroll around, and
call you after we.....do this place." The guide caromed
his eye balls at the police woman; she was quick and
adamant, and before she could have called him, he
nodded helplessly "...It is...how I earn my living..."

The three men dissolved in the bustling in random
directions, holding a piece of paper that appeared an
advertising pamphlet with "Anutaapa" written on it in
Hindi, Urdu, and Persian. Most of the walls were
plain except a few engraved with flowers and leaves

and nothing else. Repeating the same process of scrutinizing again and again, Audin had scanned a ten meter wall in fifteen minutes to an hour.

No signs of uncommonness. I need the patience of an experienced horologist. Perhaps, this is how I can define, in one aspect, the infinity- A mountain that always forces the mountaineers measuring its altitude to suicide, a meter from the zenith, out of an illusionary feeling of spiritlessness and invariability.

One of the red sandstones, the last, had a sloping surface burdened with dust. An inscription ran along its width in a wavy flow as if a right-handed person wrote with the left hand.

Large enough to hide bones!

Unfolding the pamphlet, he dabbed the dust away of the stone, and found that he was actually grating his fingers against the sharp edge of a crack, not an inscription.

Not that easy.

He turned back to find someone laughing at him; there were elephants and pigeons. The guide, with a stub like head, was nailed at Jhelum's whim.

"It is the Bajrang cannon; sixteen oxen were used to move it, second to Jahvana in strength and size.

You can read everything about them in these books to have the accurate information."

"What do 'you' know, then?"

"...I only know what I have learned, madam."

The noon was fading, and to pump their spirits up to move ahead they only had the achievement of completing Jeevan Chowk's inspection exhaustively, with no points against their name in the tally. With Jhelum denying accompanying them, the team moved through another arched entrance into another veranda for another round.

"Now we are...entering Suhat..." The gate had a dropping roof.

The architecture was similar, and this similarity was repelling and bitter, though lacking the monotonousness of the Jeevan Chowk's. It was an eighteen pillared open hall in pink surrounded by ten feet high walls, and displaying war drums and carriages.

"Here, the soldiers were briefed about...plans and strategy of the war." The hammering continued.

"I will have to have something, first, or I will faint." Rama dragged himself under the shade of a canopy as if any further jargon would make him eat the flakes of the lime-mortar on the walls. Jatharu, standing composed, had developed the appearance and numbness of sandstones like a chameleon imitates his surroundings, and showed no desires of serving the miseries of hunger or thirst. He was rather keenly interested in Audin's movements. When they all moved towards what was Rama's refuge, Jatharu asked Audin that if he had come across something incongruous, if he had any plans and strategies for rest of the journey, and if they should search together to exclude the risk of overlooking an evidence; the questions carried a padding of insecurity and precaution, in case this search becomes the survival of the fittest.

The eating outlet was modern, and offered a panoramic view of the hills apart from drinks and snacks. A motley of traditional cane chairs and stools lay on the floor in a pattern, one facing the other, that looked intentional as if to facilitate their talking.

"My nephew owns this shop." This was the guide's compelling reason for his initial haste, and called his nephew, like he was one of the richest customers himself, to present a culinary serving.

"We are moving very slowly. I would have made you familiar with everything. By this pace, you will need half a year to cover it up." He chuckled.

"Are we?"

"Sir, there was a team from the income tax department, in 1976 during the emergency, that raided the fort in suspicion of hidden treasure; even they took two months to dig the fort upside down! You should pay me at least five hundred. You are taking... too long." He sipped black syrup with a slurp matching his tone, and talked extrovertly, gaining his confidence back in absence of the police woman.

"Dug the fort? What did they dig?" All three of them, at this point of time, had not been this desperate to listen to him since morning; awestruck by the guide's words that had apparently jerked their ears.

"It was in newspapers; it was international news then." He took the last sip. "More than five hundred labourers were employed. Not a single corner was left, and they had machines. Many of the hollow walls, underground rooms, and tunnels were botched up. Nothing was found."

"Does this fort have tunnels?

"There is no scarcity. Escape tunnels out of the fort, and some of them leading to other parts within the fort. Everyone is not allowed to go in; only a few are open for tourists. That is what I said; I would have showed you everything."

What would have been intriguing to everyone else sounded a decree asking them to depart from the Jahgarh fort. The probability of locating the wall had nearly diminished; even if such a wall had existed there was no reason the treasure hunters would have spared it.

"He is an idiot; they were government hired idiots. How much constitutes the truth? Who knows? Do not think about...what is going to happen; do not stop. No ...what inspires you to stop?"

"Nothing," Audin looked up to Jatharu. "I am curious enough to know the truth." And Rama took no interest in sharing his opinion.

The three continued their search for the next seven days. They would arrive in afternoon, hire a new guide every day, and return as they had returned the day before. It was a direct call that had put to test Audin's curiosity, Rama's servility, and Jatharu's passion; while Jhelum, ignorant of what was happening around her much like a scarecrow planted at a rice paddy, was still pursuing the royal knowledge of weapons as if she was going to compensate for her less-tutored childhood.

The eighth day:

Having roped in most of the walls that were above the earth, they decided, for a change, to ransack underground tunnels that were easily accessible. Without a guiding assistant or maps, Jatharu and Audin gorged themselves in two different tunnels; Rama, feigning heat-illness, was resting at the comfortable hotel twenty kilometres away in the Jaipur city, and had bargained for a leave for the next day as well.

Audin entered a staircase leading to a narrow tunnel. A prevailing stench of urine could not be avoided. Several tourists used these secluded places, which once added to the military strength of the Jahgarh, for urination and littering. Wading through a network of plastic wrappers and peelings, reminiscent of one of those abandoned subways of Delhi, he arrived at the unvisited face of the tunnel three feet below the earth. Every tunnel was designed in such a way that after a certain distance it became pitch-dark. The width was less than two feet which discouraged the entering of multiple men simultaneously. Audin had by now covered several meters, and had switched on his defective torch to look for anything in writing. The confined walls radiated hot air stronger than a furnace, and his perspiring skin provided a hallucination of walls moving towards each other with every step. Audin could hear his lungs expanding and contracting, and the multiplied sound of his breath echoing all over. He measured the width, again, to assure himself. The passage was now sloping downwards. There was no one inviting him and no one barricading. Crossing the slope he landed in a dome that had another tunnel rising up; it was a joint; an encounter of two wildernesses. This change of geometry and spaciousness was relieving; he felt he had come out of a cupboard.

The dome was made of a carved hemisphere resting on eight stone slabs placed along the circumference whose centre was a point on the ground directly below the centre of the hemisphere.

"...uh, where am I..." He laid aside his torch, closed his eyes, and sat down. The world inside was equally dark and silent. His neck and spine had developed stiffness. The bruises on his forearms had been burning penetratingly by the surface of salty drops of sweat, and the rub of his shirt which he soon took off. He wished for an anaesthesia that could numb him.

"It has been a long time; I must go home now. I may not have done well, but there doesn't seem any other way." He looked at his watch; it was half past four. "What do I have? I am tired." He flashed his torch around, and lightened a flat wall that had clear and deep engravings. He flashed all over, and above, and on the ground. He handled his knees to stand up, and it was painful after resting for a while, and noticed the eight walls and eight engravings.

Marvellous replica, Persian, this could be the end.

He walked about the dome anonymously.

The stone measured two cross two, and the joints of limestone were thicker. He started sneezing profusely, as he zoomed in, by inhaling through his nostrils husky dust particles. He wanted to retreat swiftly but the width was a compulsory constraint. However much exhausted he was, he certainly took less time to come out. It was an orange evening. Jatharu Rishi had been waiting for him on the same bench where they had begun.

Audin entertained for a moment the desire of not revealing anything to Jatharu, not because he himself dreamt of becoming the successor – *It was the easiest way to shatter Jatharu's self-righteousness, turn him into a human again and dispatch back home,* he thought.

Audin took a few steps ahead, like a medallist, towards the open rampart in front of him - a balcony with a view to a bordering settlement of colonies touching the horizon.

The houses appear from this balcony no more than bright dots sprinkled over the entire desert; inside every house must be a frequent turmoil of opinions, of egos, of money, of power...how irrelevant it all seems from this vantage point, here. What relevance do I or Jatharu hold for someone looking at us from those tiny windows? Nothing, just some shadows.

Audin recedes towards Jatharu and reveals everything, standing akimbo, the blood circulation in his body still speedy.

"It is there, in Persian."

"What? You have found it? Come..." Jatharu left the bench, and then bent over to see Audin's answering face. A childlike agility struck him as Audin replied affirmatively.

"Did it match?"

"Yes."

"... It had to be!" The blowing air in the veranda evaporated the moisture on Audin's body, and left a cooling effect. "Where is your shirt?"

"Oh..., in there, forgot...we'll get it tomorrow," Audin could recall that checked shirt, left in the backyard last time, was also unpicked, and must have grown mouldy, "We'll undoubtedly come tomorrow, with a few tools. There is no security in here. And we'll try to remove that stone, and see. And get the shirt too."

"Victory is there for those whose heart has stationed God. How can we get defeated?" He could not stop himself from posting a Sanskrit verse.

"You have declared yourself victorious already?"

The tourists had left. The museum guards were waiting for Jhelum to close the book.

"May I know when we shall leave?" Audin said to Jhelum.

"Fifteen minutes; I am reading about Aurangzeb's cannon foundry. I must complete. I have already learned firing and loading."

"We have found it."

"That stone. Anutaapa?"

"Yes."

"Take this back then." She returned her copy of the pamphlet, crumpled as an exploited tissue paper.

Jatharu could not unload his mind that night, and kept arranging the scenes from the beginning, when he had had the first glance of the wisdom leaves, to the latest day. He could not credit himself for anything, but he had to else he would have gotten sick of watching Audin sail away the boat, and assured himself before shutting his eyes.

"It is because of me, the master, because of my blessings he has found the wall."

The ninth day:

The time they had had was not sufficient to obtain mechanically fit tools from the city market; however, they could succeed in pilfering out from the hotel, and buying from the neighbouring shops a rusty flat iron bar, a steel knife, and a pestle.

Audin had scratched off an inch deep mortar out of the joint. The knife had already bent on one side yielding to the prejudiced effects of abrasion. The depth was unknown, and there were three sides left yet to face the knife. Jatharu held the torch, the same way Rama had held it in the backyard.

"Why...do we... have secrets...always buried?"

"Hold. Hold for a while... give it to me."

Jatharu took the charge, and pummelled the pestle on the iron bar to scrape the chips off of the mortar which he judged was the efficient way, "It will...take time, it will...it is rock. You must do it...like this...if you want to do afresh..." Now, holding the torch appealed to him more efficient.

"I will." Audin gripped the tools more robotically this time, and began harassing the stone by a never ending force.

These bones are to fix the mysterious jigsaw. A heap of bones. I have spent half of my life advocating the opposite. I know what I am doing. It will steady my rocking boat, and let it sail steadily afterwards. A heap of bones.

The focus of his eyes was so channelled that he must have covered them with imaginary blinders.

Keeping in mind the prisoners to be buried alive, and to create an infallible trap, each wall was built to bear the bolt of a herd of elephants.

"If we can stay here, till tomorrow morning, we are going to slice it out."

He worked to nearly tearing his arm muscles. The inappropriateness of the tools had mercilessly increased the labour. The pummelling did not cease, the artificial lightening outside was being plugged off by the caretakers, the nocturnal animals were starting their day, and the Jahgarh fort was a despot for the next twelve hours. The breeze that was blowing outside in orphanhood was organising itself in whirls to whistle in the tunnel, but could not really deter the miners that were determined to shake the roots of the Jahgarh fort.

"That guide, we met that day, said they are a thousand year old."

"Mountain forts are invincible; they sustain for that time. Vedas have mentioned this."

"However staunch an atheist I may be, I can never equal your obsession with Vedas." he wiped the tickling sweat off his nose.

"Your mere presence here owes to my obsession. You are fortunate to have...my supervision, if you don't deny that." Jatharu spoke in an ease that was indifferent to the heat around Audin, and the stone. Audin could sense the impression of the tip of a new argument that Jatharu was steering to, and toiling for eight hours, he was too weak to debate. Afterwards was a deliberate silence.

It was seven o'clock, after the sunrise, when all the four sides had developed cracks which were absorbing every speck of the light of the torch. The sleep deprived eyes of Audin at last felt worthwhile, and peeped in. The stone lay mortar-less, but resisted to get evacuated from its rightful residence. He pushed the iron rod in and out and in every dimension that could displace the devil. Jatharu, whose heart was pumping more blood than ever, and whose growing impatience was stalking Audin, made sure by his advice that it did not fall inside on the bones.

After the skilful negotiation of attacks, he safely abled the stone to fall on the heap of limestone debris, like a toppled drawer. Jatharu, ambushed for the moment, pushed Audin. "No! Do not go in! Step back! I must go in; step back, I am the....God-send." With his torso filling up the cubical space, he shouted again, "Show me the lights! Where are you lost?" and pushed himself in like a four-legged man. Audin entered after handling the torch.

It was a spacious chamber, and only a chamber of bricks. There was no sign of life or death. Below their soles was the desert sand, and their feet danced about every atom but could not find the bones. None had been there.

"Give me the torch! I want it!"

"You have it...in your hand..."

"Where are his bones? They are nowhere! I am not a street wandering juggler who can be deceived. I am never wrong! Where are they?" His eyebrows strained his forehead.

"You are losing yourself. Let us go out. It is all empty. We did what we could."

"Who is responsible for this?" The anger transformed into disappointment, for he had nothing to curse, neither his "Golden" fate nor "Absolutely" truthful Vedas.

"No one. They must have gotten decomposed. He was a normal human, if he ever existed; mortal like us. Let us go out."

"Where are the others? The other graves?"

"They are connected; it is a circular room, of nothing but sand."

"I cannot believe! I cannot have these countenances of patience that you are flaunting!"

"That is so because you have been falsified. That is the reason. I am not flaunting."

"Oh! You must celebrate then; I have been falsified by a man who is half my age!"

"Even I did not want to end it this way. I am disappointed, for both of us. Rishi ji, I am helpless."

The gates of the gilded fort had opened, to once again welcome the newly landed tourists and to exile those who have gone beyond the land, unnecessarily far, and unnecessarily deep.

Jatharu and Audin reached the museum, to look for Jhelum who had not arrived yet. Silently leaning against the parapet, their eyes patrolled the all-pervading Aravallies, as if they were strangers meeting for the first time.

"What would you do now?" Jatharu asked, agreeing to himself that he had been harsh on Audin, and his virtues.

"I will go back home. Whatever time I have spent with you, in your ashram, and this fort, is memorable. It was a good, and a diverse, experience."

"... yet even I have learned from you,"

"What is that?"

"The art of neutrality..."

"I believed it annoyed you. I have, and I will if you don't emphasize that again." Audin smiled.

"When did you come to India?"

"Twenty years back; my forefathers had settled in India."

"And Rama? You are a very close friend of Rama?"

"We are school friends. Almost the same time."

"Twenty years..."

"Did not he try to convert you to theism?"

"No, he offered his teachings. Whatever you preached to him, in fact. And it is never about conversion. It is about conviction. You are very convinced with Vedas, which is why I am now disappointed for you. I will go back and re-start this. I had nothing to lose, but whatever you preached, and trusted to be absolute truth, is now eclipsed by something. I can understand that. It is like... suddenly, one comes to know that the gemstones he has been accumulating throughout his life have been declared as pebbles...Isn't it?"

Jhelum interrupted, "Did you stay here last night?"

"Yes. But I am empty-handed; couldn't get the bones. I will leave for Delhi today; I will talk to Rama. When do you think?"

"I will need a week more. I can come on my own." She showed a book. "This may be useful to you, written by Aurangzeb; it has some relevant information."

"Thank you." He accepted the present. "I will see to it in the evening," unaware that it had been sneaked out from the shelf.

After spending eight hours in the sleeping bout, Audin woke up smearing the white bed sheet in physical fatigue and dashing hopes. The curtains were drawn. Rama stood in the flowery balcony outside the hotel room. Audin followed the trail from where was coming nature's inspiration. He had not talked to him much lately.

"You look disturbed. How is your illness? I am not demanding an embarrassing explanation for this situation. You have indeed helped me, Rama. Failure, or success, is often dependent on chance- outcome of the mixture of circumstances that you have created. Chances have great importance." Rama was chawing a handful of dried gram. He chawed sluggishly, and carried the eternal boredom of a man at the end of a mile long queue. "Hmm, I am well. There is nothing to worry. Jhelum said that we are going to go tomorrow?"

"Has she come? When does she want to go? Perhaps, you will have to be here."

"Yes, she is persistent; another week,"

"Where is Rishi ji?"

"...meditating."

Singing the same song of the Beatles, almost nothing else to do, he threw his attention on a beggar who was accosting someone in the street buying from a puppet shop.

The beggar, like a convention, unfurled his amputated hands to foreigners, and for Indians recited the names of Hindu Gods in addition. This chore of his invited Audin to say something, and he said, to himself:

Chances have a great importance. They justify and fit everything that is attributed to a fictitious destiny. Was it his destiny or the result of diligent hard work? If it was hard work, why then did not he receive the alms on every occasion, and if it is his "destiny" why does he have to work hard? None of these. Chances, chances have a great importance.

Having observed the street end to end, Audin was eager to meet Jatharu and to know if he was pacified enough for the return journey. His eagerness stumbled upon Jhelum's book- "The Letters from Aurangzeb" lying unattended on the travel bag, and plucked it up.

Jatharu rubbed his palms, and then placed them over his eyelids; this he did repeatedly and artfully. Audin knew it was soothing, and he did not desire to alarm him. Meanwhile, sitting idly on the cushy chair, the cover-page of the book looked decent to be explored; it had a detailed and colourful painting of

Aurangzeb – A side view of a frowning face, and a pen. Inside it, a doubly folded page, a token by Jhelum, took Audin to the middle of the book that displayed a printed copy of a letter dated to 1659 A.D.

The letter read as follows:

"I, Alamgir, declare that my brother, Dara Shukoh! Is the ally of infidels! Treacherous to the state, he has spat on my face by dishonouring my strict orders of burial of captured Brahmins, and their leader – Anutaapa! Providing refuge to them in his own place of stay! The clergy has declared his acts as acts of betrayal to the religion! He must be beheaded along with the Brahmins, today evening! And his body be paraded through the streets on a female elephant! Anutaapa, whom the idolaters call their saviour, must be flogged to death too! His body be flayed from a sharp sword heinously! And then be chained on floor of the sewage tank of the fort to rot in my urine and faeces! The justice be done!

Praise be to All Mighty!

Praise be to All Mighty!"

The chest had been flung open all over again. Audin read it word by word, like it was his own obituary delivered beforehand. Rama came in absent-mindedly; as though chawing had overpowered his brain, and said, "Wha..., mmm." He mumbled as he couldn't move his tongue, submerged in the truckload of grams.

"Read this."

He held the book upside down, then held it otherwise, and after reading for a while, said, "Astonishing, I say chances do have a great importance, you must go, or you will regret it all your life. One last time; you must go."

Audin's intelligence was now like an exhausted deer's who was chasing a watery reflection on a hot summer to only know that it was a mirage.

"Is there a chance that the bones will not have decomposed by now? Or eroded by water? Is it possible? Is it not irrational to follow a random history book?" Audin asked.

"Rational or irrational, whatever it may be. Plug the last hole. One last time..."

"...are you coming?" Rama took too long a time to respond explicitly, as if the question sought the causes of origin of this universe. The slack in his behaviour had tightened, and he said overwhelmingly, "I would have, no doubt, Audin; it is I who have brought you to here, but I have...I have symptoms of asthmatic allergy. I must not in any case inhale dust. "

"Alright. I should have known that."

The Jahgarh fort had a total of five tanks; four supplied fresh water and one, in the north east, was the sewage tank constructed outside the boundary walls. It was a structure fifteen meters high with no separate floors and the base area nearly of that of twenty cemetery plots arranged to form a square. The section of it visible to all, symmetrical and trapezoidal, was only half of what lay below the ground. It was bonneted to the fort walls, and could only be communicated through a doorway, that opened near the foundry of the fort, and an attached staircase that led to the bottom of the tank.

The drainage system of Jahgarh fort was so scientific and organised that it functions well to date, and occasional rain water is perfectly channelled, with a high gradient, from the local drains to the main drain which then terminates into the roof of the sewage tank. It has never been repaired since the Indian archaeological department took it over on the day it was first opened for the general public.

In broad daylight, Audin and Jatharu were in front of the doorway covered by a wooden stile-like board, to wrap up the supplementary ceremony. Everything around them seemed quite tasteless – the afternoon, the fort, the tank, the doorway, and their own shadows, like someone being served a bowl of boiled spinach who had been swallowing it for the past two weeks.

The board, whose placement had a kind of an emergency onto it, could not entirely blanket the doorway. Audin pushed it aside with the same ease with which it was put. The square staircase was haunting and very deep, as though announcing that the goers would never return, and it revolved along the four walls till it touched the bottom.

Audin stepped in; the amount of light and air was fairly sufficient, for the walls had been perforated with holes at calculated distances. It was not slippery but the broad steps were greased with dead fungus all over. Along it was a brick hedge with vivid salt stains on it; this wall protected the two men from reaching the bottom in a jiffy without using the staircase.

"How many steps have we descended?"

"Twenty seven..."

The staircase turned right; the roof of the tank could now be seen. It had wide openings to sprinkle the waste slurry on the earthen meshes which were stubbed in the walls. These meshes were porous and would carry a mixture of coal ash, dung, and hay to absorb the solid particles which were later dried further and used as a fuel to the central heating system of the fort.

"When I first entered that tunnel that day, it had reeked of urine. And ironically, this place which is a sewage tank is odourless," Audin said, recalling the count of the number of steps. The position of this tank was so chosen by the designers that it gained maximum heat from the sun for most part of the day, thus the waste slurry would get its moisture readily evaporated without producing odours.

"How many steps?"

"Thirty six...We are, I think, half way down the tank. I cannot see the entryway."

The staircase had no signs of a recent human intervention, and the threads of mould on its edges and on the meshes gave the tank the dreariness of an abandoned cotton mill.

"It may be marshy. So, you haven't brought anything today?" Jatharu asked observing the battlefield at the base, standing on the last step; in a stern posture as though he had an obedient army backing him, ready and waiting for his command. The bottom of the tank had the same family of wild bushes, thorny shrubs, and low grasses that imperialized the desert. A person with a squint would have mistaken this trapezoid for a warehouse that stored dry vegetation

"I have got the plates. A stick would have been helpful; it is not marshy, though."

"Be careful; there may be desert reptilians." Thorny bushes were creeping up to waist height, and were stubborn in their pledge to guard the property. Audin elevated his vision towards the top, and felt himself to be in a huge chimney that would be diffusing green smoke. They started flattening the shrubs in opposite corners with their feet, like it was a plank for making crop circles.

"Are you apprehensive of reptiles?" Jatharu asked, trying to ensure himself of the same.

"No, uh, perhaps; I don't know. People say my reaction time is a little late, so it becomes that I don't know how to express fear, or surprise."

"But you were too fast in winding everything up; should have brought something, at least those tools!"

"I should have brought Bhola Prasad; he is a gardener. He would have scythed this away in one stroke." This flavoured his face with a nostalgic amusement.

"Have you been to such a place before; chimneys? Around the village?" Audin asked, keeping himself in motion. There was no reply. Audin asked again, but Jatharu's reaction time had surpassed his. "Hmm?" Audin turned back towards Jatharu. "It looks like you stamped a reptile?" Jatharu did not move. Audin went closer, and looked over Jatharu's shoulder to find where he had been stuck.

There laid an ugly termite mound risen, about a feet high, on the bushy ground. Snaky creepers were swirling around something that appeared to be the leg bone of a human. Along with the creepers were snuggled iron chains that had held a "dead" body.

This is who I am; Jatharu, the acclaimed sage, is going to be the new successor of the world! The controller of this Earth! I had known it! I had known it! I have overpowered the ordeal! The fruits have ripened; I will be glorified as the Apaursheya! This sinner who was running parallel to me, who pitied on me and my wisdom, has been shown the mirror; a pawn who will polish the horses of my chariot!

"It is a dead body!" Audin reacted; unintentionally counter attacking Jatharu's pride.

"Hand me the leaves! The plates! The bones! I can see them with my eyes! I have got them in my eyes! I want the wisdom leaves!" Jatharu exclaimed, without looking back, fearing that he might lose their sight.

"I am...I am on the leaves. I have seen...dead bodies before." Audin had started feeling a little colder.

"Give me! Do not chatter!"

The skeleton had a preserved layer of flesh on it that may have been due to the slowed down, or rather inactivated, decomposition process; his nose, which once would have been long and pointed, was clay-like and flaky; the eyes were sunken deep but calm as if they knew what was going around; the withered dreadlocks whose roots could be seen in the skull had encroached the vicinity like a communicable disease had sneaked into the bushes.

"Here, the leaves." Audin came forward. "Wait! Uh! I! I saw, I saw him breathing! I..." Audin's own breath was now speeding up. "I saw the chest moving!"

"It cannot!"

Jatharu squatted to examine the fossil. The recognition of being a human was lacking; it was camouflaged with the macabre torture that had once nipped off his life little by little.

Of course, it cannot decompose before the arrival of the fifth element.

"You are getting on to it; I did! I did see the chest moving!" Audin experienced a feeble up-thrust, a sense of tangible coldness around his groin.

Jatharu held the leaves in his right hand and chanted the Sanskrit hymn vigorously and blindly. When a few minutes of rhythmic sound had gone past his ears the apparently dead man sighed, and started to speak in sighs, "You took too long, Dara Shukoh. You took too long, but you have kept your five hundred year old promise you made to your friend, Anutaapa. The promise of restoring the leaves to the Apaursheya. "

If raising of the hair epitomizes ghastliness, it will be said without a doubt that every hair on Audin's body had ghastly erected to a stiffness that it was pulling away to peel the skin off. Jatharu Rishi was running out of life, for his head went heavy; the heaviness of blood clogging and seeping.

Audin, shivering, lost control over his bladder, and passed the body fluids uncontrollably, and with the fluids had passed the anecdotes of atheism, the power of logics, the demand of evidences, and the reactionlessness.

"Audin, I am your friend. You have talked to me before many times. You have forgotten me, my friend. When you were sitting on your throne and your court men called you the King Aurangzeb. Do not fear. Every moment that you have lived had to be so, for there were many men whom you had to make a part of your life, whom you had to partake with the fruits of action. I had to lose my wisdom leaves, I had to suffer this confinement of shackles, to punish one and to reward the other, and I had to let this happen. Men may come and go. The belief may shrink and spread. The theories may bud and wither. You may accept or reject. But the absolute truth is the absolute truth."

Anutaapa touched his wisdom leaves, freed himself from the shackles, his hunch back was recovering, and walked up the staircase to reign over the Earth, to complete the tenure left.

Chapter 10

~~~

1659 A.D.

Anutaapa, in the nine thousandth century of his reign but yet youthful, was leading his life of seclusion in the valleys of deciduous forests of the Aravallies. He spent most of his time wandering the nearby villages falling in the boundaries of Aurangzeb's empire, though he used to retire himself every night in his hut under a berry tree. It was the last day before the night of the full moon, and a coterie of three Brahmins, who had learned about Anutaapa's identity, was to arrive here to meet him, as they did every month. With the break of the dawn, he had begun meditating, having blocked all the openings of the body- eyes, nose, ears, mouth, and the lower passages, to experience the brief amalgamation of his inner self with the ether of the Universe. This was an unvarying practice to embark upon the day; after this he released himself, and gradually re-appeared in the Earthly realm- a realm of sorrow and misery, and soon this fact got demonstrated with apparent pre-planned timing. Anutaapa heard, from his purified ears, a distant wailing of men and women in the forest. A few miles from his hut had lived a tribal family of ten. At once he ran, at an alarming pace, towards the source of the cries, clutching the wisdom leaves.

A blazing red fire had charred the trees and huts to grey ashes. It was passionately engulfing whatever came its way. A helpless girl, her legs covered in flames, was fluttering like a featherless bird, shrieking out for her dear life. Anutaapa summoned the clouds to come into sight and water down the fires to extinction. Who possessed the courage to disobey the Apaursheya? It was a downpour. No one but the girl could be saved.

"There are medicinal herbs on the bank of "Srivat" Lake in the forest. Prepare unction; you will be healed." Anutaapa decided to leave. The girl erupted into tears.

"What had to happen has happened. Do not lament."

"There is nobody left." She covered her face, and deeply sobbed.

"You have to complete your demarked period in this form of life."

"What have I done? Why should I stay alive? ...to bear this pain?"

Anutaapa recollected the past actions of the aggrieved girl that were responsible for this day and said, "You were a landlord in Laikhat village, thousands of years ago; time has come for penances; not a sin can go unchecked! You had conspired against a poor farmer, and scalded him and his family to death with your brothers as accomplices. But the farmer survived; so have you. He lived the rest of his life in bereavement; so will you. This is the law of nature. I had healed him, so have I healed you. You may accept or reject."

"O young man! I don't understand your confusing words. You have saved me from this fire; you must help me lead this paralysed life too!"

"A group of Brahmins is about to arrive at my hut; you can take refuge in their village, and take up your new life."

The Brahmins were standing outside his hut. They bowed down all together as they saw Anutaapa coming. They possessed fraught expressions in their gestures which overruled the surprise they had to see the girl in company.

"How are you? And your preaching?"

"We are in trouble, each one of us. O Mahatma! Our Saviour! The King Aurangzeb has kept a reward of five hundred gold coins on the head of every Brahmin, and his army will be invading the nine villages day after tomorrow. Save our lives, and our religion! You can incinerate him and his men by merely looking at them. Help us!"

"That is injustice to the king."

The Brahmins were taken aback, "You are the sole hope. O great sage! His cruelty does not define justice. You are the knower of Vedas; how can you back his deeds?"

"Undoubtedly, it is injustice to you as well, but, Aurangzeb has conquered this throne by defeating your king in the battlefield. A sage cannot interfere with the duties of the fighting class of men and disrupt the divisions of the society. A king can only be dethroned by another passionate king. I can incinerate him in moments, but that is against the path of righteousness."

"How can, then, you tolerate him deviating from the path of righteousness?"

"He is certainly not following the kingship duties except for his self-satisfying motives. Do not worry; rest for a while. I will discuss with you the strategies, today, that you must follow for integrity of the kingdom, and only you have to follow. Tomorrow morning, you will depart from here and I will accompany you on your way to your village."

The Brahmins showed diffidence in enquiring about the identity of the girl, and that how could she stay with them. "As you command. I may falter in words... pardon my asking about the presence of this girl; I am not able to understand by my timid intelligence."

"She is a tribal girl who lost her family in the forest fires in the morning. I have accepted her as my daughter. You will refuge her in your village, and as her father I request you to educate her according to her intelligence, and find her a suitable groom for a household life."

The girl, who was patiently hearing the conversation, said unhesitatingly, "How can I be your daughter, young man? I cannot be."

The Brahmins looked at each other, and then looked at Anutaapa to intervene who at once observed the girl's proceedings, and said, "You are keenly attracted to my material body. Do not! I am a celibate. You are committing another sin!"

"I have already accepted you as my groom. I will marry you, or die!"

"O thoughtless girl! Cloak your lusty mind! I warn you, I am your well-wisher. Do not compel me to curse you to sullen your immoral intention."

The Brahmins unanimously hushed her to go away, "O fallen girl! It is to your good, going away. Casting lusty eyes on a celibate is unforgivable! Go away! You have lost your family; indulge yourself in pious activities!"

"I will not fall prey to your ploy. I will not step away!"

Anutaapa reached for one of the leaves to curse the girl forever, but he could not. He was about go back on his eighth vow he made to his master Paramhamsa.

You must not use the divine power of wisdom leaves on others for your own self, unless unavoidable, and with keen judgment.

It was indeed avoidable. He neither put his hand away, nor cursed the girl. He cursed himself, and transformed into a surly hunched back human, with patched hair and dappled skin. The youth and the beauty that the girl was entranced to now disgusted her.

"No! You have humiliated me! You have deceived me! You will have to pay for this! You had lured me into your charm. You will have to repay!" She could not control herself, ran away, and got lost in the woods. Her utterance could still be heard after she left.

The Brahmins, initially, seemed to have been disturbed by her rebellious demand.

"I am bound by my duty, and my vows. I cannot forget my master's words under any circumstance." Anutaapa exemplified once again his ability to discern the right from the wrong, and to strike a balance between the adversity and the use of the power.

As the dusk set in, the army men had, without waiting for the next day, invaded the villages in search of Brahmins and temples; five hundred gold coins seemed too easy for a Brahmin's life. The soldiers were laddering to the temple tops hammering down the structures, and a few without weapons were loading the sacks on donkeys with accumulated debris for pavement construction. The Earthly idols were reduced to shards, and those precious ones of gold and silver were plundered and sent to the fort's vault. The Brahmins found preaching in the temple were captured and their heads were barbarously cut off. The torsos were scattered all around the streets, on temple stairs, and in the drains, like dead fallen leaves of autumn. After attacking the temples they moved their horses to find those who did not conduct the temple services and were commonly revered as the elevated ones; the three who were safely resting in Anutaapa's hut.

A Brahmin's house was easy to separate out; their walls bore the religious marks and symbols.

"Tell me where has he hidden? Or I shall send you and your children for serfdom!" The commander, Bahadur Khan, sitting astride on the horse, held the Brahmin's wife by her hair. "Tell me where the idolatrous is! I will cut your throat, too!" after dragging her on the street to and fro; when she had fallen loose, he roared again, "Show me your senseless tongue!"

Horses' hooves were stained in blood, and so were the swords. Children who had not seen such a sight in their short lives could not understand anything, and only shivered. The mother, who introduced to them this world as a peaceful creation of God, was helplessly asking them to run inside.

"He has gone to the forest."

Bahadur khan vaunted the sword. "Where in the forest?"

"...in the forest, I don't know....they have gone to meet the sage. I know nothing else! Leave us! Have mercy! Fear God!"

"That sage! Your saviour! None will be spared! You all will be put to death!" He slashed her throat, splashing the blood right on the face of her children.

The commander made it clear, loudly, to the soldiers that the three Brahmins have gone into hiding in the forest, hiding behind their sorcerous patron, and they have to hand him over alive to the king for the privileged beheading. And without affording a second thought, the soldiers loosened the reins, and headed for the bait.

The deciduous forest, in the night, had become impenetrable. A bright cresset, at this hour, would have helped them distinguish between the ways and the thorny trees, but the passionate soldiers did not care, for they were to protect their state from the infidels and their leaders; the horses, though, were pricked all over on their shoulders and flanks by the thorns as if they were being extruded through a market of porcupines.

"Should not we wait for the morning? It is complete dark." A soldier sanely asked to Bahadur Khan.

"Who are you? Impotent! You will be trampled ahead of them if you recite your cowardice again!" Bahadur Khan came in madly, "Whoever dares to go against me, I will bury him at this soil. We shall divide in five units, from here, and besiege the forests. We shall alight from our horses now and march forward! For infidels might hear the gallops and run away! Hold your spears!"

Anutaapa, and the Brahmins, were asleep, clueless, in the hut, and outside was the tribal girl preparing herself to intrude. The night was peaceful. She entered in with the same surreptitiousness as she had seen in her father while attacking an unconcerned deer. Her revengeful eyes were looking for Anutaapa, who got himself easily recognized with his shining leaves and the hunched back. She sat beside him, and observed his body. Then observed his kamandala (the wooden vessel), and began excreting in and around it. Polluting the sacred reminiscent of Anutapa's master's fatherly touch, she glanced at the shining leaves and tore the sacred thread off. The eternal wisdom leaves which the tribal girl blamed to be the cause of her misery, and which he had been protecting for years, were in vulnerable hands.

Bahadur khan and his unit had at the same time found the hut, which they believed to be of some tribal inhabitants who could have refuged the Brahmins, and were moving forward with spears pointing at every straw that made the hut. The girl came out, unaware of these intruders, and ran, which naturally tipped the soldiers off. A hurled spear thrust into her ankle, and she keeled over, and could not get up; ironically, like the unconcerned deer of his surreptitious father's hunt. She whined and whined to numb the pain, and did not stop. A few soldiers plunged forward and snatched away the shining object.

"She is a woman!" They shouted.

Anutaapa woke up, and reached for his kamandala. What he could only find was the inauspiciousness. His sacred thread was loosely swirling on his shoulder. The Brahmins told him about hearing the whine of a girl. Anutaapa had already figured out what would have happened. He sat mediating at once to locate where the wisdom leaves were, but could not, and he knew he cannot.

The wisdom leaves cannot be determined by clairvoyance; no yogi can locate them exercising his occult powers, not even in his dreams.

They came out, and found themselves besieged.

"Here are they! Hiding! Chain these saffron-clad devils!" the commander ordered. He was surprised to see the hunched back man with the three Brahmins. "Who is that man? A sacrifice for your demonic sorceries? No one can save you from the mighty sword of the king!"

"He is a sorcerer. He is the leader of all. He has converted himself into this form by magic. This shining object is magical. Do what you want to do to them. Spare my life! I don't belong to any one of them." The girl pleaded from the ground.

"This object is of no use to you. I will surrender myself and return it, I am your well-wisher." Anutaapa was being chained, like an ordinary prisoner, along with the three. "Bahadur Khan! We are ready to sacrifice ourselves under your swords, but do not think of him as worldly! He is a saint! It will not be good for you and your irreligious king Aurangzeb!"

"Slit his tongue! At this moment! He will never utter the name of our emperor with such disgrace."

Thereafter, the girl was assaulted playfully with spears and was left to live a handicapped life in the forest forever. The Brahmins were beaten, and loaded on the horses as the debris, before the army made for the Jahgarh fort.

Prince Dara Shukoh, elder brother of Aurangzeb, was standing alone in the balcony of Suhat Niwas twiddling with the carved flowers on pillars; sleepless and helpless for the whimsical mass-murdering of Brahmins today. Dara was liberal-minded, and a compassionate of Brahmins. He had been so fascinated by the Vedic literature that he had covertly arranged for the translation of most of it into Persian.

Bahadur Khan entered to reveal the good news, and have his rewards.

"The infidels have been killed, and their leaders captured! As was the order! O great prince!" The soldiers dragged in the Brahmins burdened in chains. Dara Shukoh, pitying himself, could not meet their eyes and kept looking at the white moon who became the mediator of the talks, as Dara said to it, "Prison... them, and bring them to the court of the emperor tomorrow morning...You will get your bounty."

One of the Brahmins appealed, "We may be beheaded tomorrow morning, but you must protect the wisdom leaves that Bahadur khan has seized; they belong to this sage and must be restored, no matter how. You are a learned man; you must know what you are doing."

Dara Shukoh turned his gaze towards Anutaapa, who was smiling patiently. Anutaapa turned towards the moon and said, "You, and your brother, are a part of my long journey,"

Next morning, the court had set in. The emperor Aurangzeb, satisfied to the core of his heart, sat on his peacock throne, with his "wise" court-men lined on both sides. The killing of the idolaters in such a huge number had puffed their faces with pride except Dara Shukoh's, who was fading in humiliation.

"Cover this grotesque animal! How nauseating he is!" Aurangzeb disdainfully frowned at Anutaapa's presence. The court-men, who were previously laughing at his bodily appearance, too, began feeling the nausea after the king's first reaction.

"Pardon me! O great emperor! This animal is the leader of infidels! We have captured him alive, and these three, from the forest. They had been conspiring against you!" Bahadur Khan could not wait for long to narrate his prowess. "And I have this present for you! This golden ornament! The infidels revere this as mystical. It will adorn the foot-rest of your throne. Please accept it." He came forward, and bowed down being an equal commander of flattery.

"You expect me to go near this ugly man? Devil! Take them out of the court! And behead them in line before the next meal!"

"O protector of faith! Alamgir! Such an easy death! I will personally see that these men who are propagators of false religion are tortured! And tortured to death! To set an example, so nobody can dare to lead the infidels again! I will, myself, bury them alive! Let justice be done to the faith!" Dara Shukoh stood up from his seat.

"Let justice be done! Bury them! And do what my knowledgeable brother says!"

Bahadur Khan pulled the chains. A few court-men hurried to take the opportunity of kicking them as if it was a sacred ritual. Dara Shukoh ran to pretend as the in-charge of the execution, and held Anutaapa's hand, and whispered in his disfigured ears, "I promise you, I will return the wisdom leaves to you, whatever it takes."

After two months, Dara Shukoh's plans for rescuing Anutaapa were revealed, and he was publically executed along with his son, and he took the unkept promise to his grave. Anutaapa, despite Aurangzeb's repeated efforts, could not be killed for he was uncompromisingly blessed with a lifetime of ten thousand years.

Thank You

Jacqueline Baron McCue – for that encouragement.

Abhas Sinha – for not giving a second thought about designing the cover; for staying up till early mornings to help me have a fantastic, painting-esque cover.

Shivabagh – Rohit, Pankaj, Rachit, Tarun, Vaibhav, and Nipun – for having faith in me; for letting me write every night there in 101; for the half-finished book trailer. Rajyasabha – Hitesh, Arihant, Akant, Mukul, Ravi, Saurabh, Nitin, Sandeep – for being there; Vinit & Ashutosh – for bringing that precious book.

My wife, Deepti – for endless support; for allowing me to re-write in the spare time only meant to be spent with the family.

My parents – for every little thing.

I owe this novel to Nipun Chawla who listened to every sentence before, and after, it got typed.

About The Author

Ashish Laxman spent the early adult years of his life with numerous ascetics in Hebri, Vrindavan, and Uttarakhand. In the past, he worked as a Mechanical engineer, and as an  Analyst. Now, a full-time teacher, the author shares most of his time with school children. He can be found reading or writing stories in the forests of the Northern Ridge, Delhi.

This book won him the National Debut Youth Fiction Award in 2013.

Have an opinion about this book? Share it with the author:

ashishdaslaxman@gmail.com